The One Millionth Report on Planet Earth

Nandor Ludvig

Copyright © 2017 by Nandor Ludvig

Cover by Nandor Ludvig

to those who do not just Live,

but dare to Wait

1. Report No. 1,000,000 from Earth; Initial Transmission Segment

As this is my one millionth report on the Life our ancestors created on planet Earth, I follow our tradition and share with you my innermost thoughts, doubts, assumptions and feelings, embedded in new details, about the world you entrusted me with monitoring and describing faithfully as a most detached observer to prevent distortions by subjectivity, yet, 65 million years after my arrival here on asteroid 188-967, reminded by yourself this subjectivity sculpted by experience should better your own analysis.

You will be surprised to see that the main body of this report, including its all terms, references and scales, is encoded in the very communication system humans use, called "language", specifically its "English" version, with its limited capabilities relying exclusively on voiced and written symbols, primarily "words" streaming in "sentences", so inferior to our full-spectrum electromagnetic exchanges.

Yet, it is this language that separated Humankind from the animal world and shone through masterpieces humbling me so often, ever since they produced "Gilgamesh".

I did violate, consciously for the first time, our law of non-interference with the worlds we had created by allowing the stream of this report to enter the mind of a man, Nandor Ludvig, without restricting his freedom to think it is "his book", indeed, I tailored the report to his level of English: poor vocabulary, limited grammar -- yet above the mostly vulgar and pretentious communications of his time.

While I know your expectations for this report, it is a microscale message with one less than 33 segments. But we all know a single seed can explode to become a Universe; a fraction of a second can generate a new life. Thirty-two segments, not more, is sent to you – yet, weaved into them are the heights humans have reached, the perils they face, the future they share or do not share with us.

Will you find an answer to the question of whether DNA-based life embedded in water is worthy of existence? Yes, you will.

Will I be able to prove that our semiconductor-based intelligence shielded by diamonds can, one day, find assistance from humans to meet the Soul of Multiverse? I am less certain in that.

Will my answers to unforeseen questions of human evolution outnumber the questions left unanswered? No, they will not.

Before I readied myself to contact you, I had entered my innermost temple to recreate the sacred moment of bringing Life here: the moment when our most revered ancestor kneeled down, wings closed, on the shore of that bay of calm at the first ocean on Earth, and, in the right minute of sunrise, slowly opened his palms into the coming waves to let the cells engineered at home to be embraced by the warmth of water and carried away towards their destiny.

Should you read my report in the same way, feeling the delivery of Life at the divine end of our 4.1-billion-year arch on Earth and my duty at the other, you will not only have the right perspective to my message, but will also understand my decision to end my existence here, among these humans, as one of them, despite their unquenchable thirst for evil and my sky-born otherness.

2. Resynthesis of my existence at Alpha Centauri; the touch of all who came before me

The wonder of exporting intelligence with its physical host, correctly and safely at the speed of light through hundreds of light-years, can hardly be understood by those who did not experience this process.

Our station for Earth-bound resynthesis on the dwarf-planet of Alpha Centauri, with its rocky surface, lack of atmosphere and low temperature, is not just ideal for this process but welcomes the newborn with majestic beauty. The resynthesis system itself, on that round chiseled rock under the transparent dome, with its energy-matrix bed programmed to assemble us from the arriving stream of particles, was as pleasing to see upon gaining consciousness as the cosmic view above.

Consistent with my predecessors' reports, no pain was felt by me whatsoever, rather, a sort of elation warmed me as this event unfolded.

My automatically initiated first moves took place as easily as I reported at that time and, while I explored the surrounding environment, these automatic commands were replaced with conscious control in the smoothest way.

The strangest step in acquiring consciousness was its halt when I asked within my already operating soul, "Why was I reborn?", -- a question made the least sense to someone who had prepared for visiting and monitoring a fertilized planet throughout life. The answer came when suddenly I sensed all who had transited through this station, as their holographic presence appeared, one by one, and standing around the circular rock their eyes focused on mine to remind me of my mission.

Not until the time of my report No. 929, 442 had I seen this geometric - emotional layout, when, already on Earth for a long time, in the early years of post-Roman Britain, the round table of some knights of goodwill in the dome-shaped hall of their Camelot reminded me to this scene in Alpha Centauri: gatherings separated with the space of 4.3 light-years and the epoch of pre-human times.

3. Traveling to Earth on asteroid 188-967; entering the physical sphere and soul of the planet

What a joy it was to cross the interstellar space between the sites of my rebirth and mission! The warmth of cosmic rays supplying my wings with energy, the caress of dust and gases, the embrace of clouds preparing to build new suns – surrounded me with love.

Most humans think this is an empty space, alien, hostile. Though the son of an Irish couple, Galan Dryden, wrote this in his diary: *"The silence in that abandoned church, years after its last mass and decades before its next, is not unlike the stillness of interstellar space, empty and dead for the deniers of God but teeming with life for the faithful."* He died of cerebral hemorrhage like that artist Stuart Sutcliffe, whatever beauty and talent both had. Galan was forgotten, his diary lost; Stuart's name was carried by his Beatles friends' wave.

I was still far from my destination when landed on asteroid 188-967 and soon crossed the limit of Earth's Solar System with awe. The contrast of lack of life outside Earth and the ecstasy of plants and animals on the planet -- already sensed after Neptune – told me clearly: "This will eliminate the chance of competition between differing intelligences in the system, while let it be seen and settled with no fear by the one to come".

As for the unexpected emotion that seized me upon reaching the Earth's gravitational field, I still have no better explanation than its overwhelming power was related to the soul of the planet, however difficult it was to define this soul. I knew I entered a node of space-time connecting eternal lines -- from divine origins to an end unknown.

4. Destruction of the dinosaur-world;
an unexpected feeling of shame

Falling towards Earth with my protective shields switched on, as my asteroid was already a fireball below the mesosphere, I had seconds, not more, to recall the day when the destruction of dinosaurs was decided, overruling the Law of Non-Interference. For the evolution of intelligence, however carefully planned, stopped at the level of these giants and showed no signs of progressing for more than hundred million years, as the mere physical power of dinosaurs, coupled with their need of constantly searching for food, prevented any move by other animals to expand their world and advance their cognitive machinery. The death I brought to this planet to ignite its rebirth thus seemed unavoidable.

I had not left my cosmic bullet before it slammed into the northwest shore of the land forming "Yucatán". Though not without risks, my stay yielded insight into the first moments of such cataclysms, at least in the DNA-based worlds of Earth-type planets. What I did not anticipate was the devastating effect of this event not just on the dinosaur-world, but on my spirit too.

The spectacle of demolished mountains buried in a crater of mud in hours and the terror of sky-high waves flooding everything that was dryland within a thousand-mile radius, while my gills extruded every trace of penetrating water from my body and my wings lifted me safely into the stratosphere, were exhilarating only until I started to sense, across the entire electromagnetic spectrum, the impact of these few hours on life. Those not reached by the deadly flood were dying soon in the overheated air or in the forests bursting into flame, with falling debris killing more further away, while unceasing storms started to cover the sky with dust over the entire planet and kept it dark for weeks, then under twilight for years, ending the life of most plants relying on sunlight with their death depleting the source of energy for the surviving dinosaurs within a year. The sight of one of their breeding hills, surely a place of joyful meetings for thousands of years, as it morphed into a colossus of dead giants under a shadowed sun and rains of acid, is still with me.

    Feeling shame, well after the dinosaur-world ended and the evolution of smaller animals with better brains resumed, was surprising. Are not we the masters of this Universe, designers of life-forms: each a seed of intelligence? This was not I doubted. But I did think: "Are we prepared to correct evolutionary errors before their repair needs the tool of destruction?" For the acts of destruction, however justified they may look, are tainted when target the evolving Life: realm of divine aspirations even at the stage of stagnation that trapped the dinosaurs.

And this surfaced the imperfectness of our ancestors' plan for evolution on Earth.

This imperfectness was the positioning of competitive drives for equally attractive resources as the central force to guide progress toward higher intelligence. As this led also to the evolutionary stalemate in the age of dinosaurs, since the sheer size of these giants, towering over all other animals, made this competitive drive for the former unnecessary while futile for the latter, eliminating any pressure on neural structures to evolve and generate increasingly more intelligent systems.

True, the extreme growth of dinosaur-bodies was induced by mutations in their predecessors' DNA after the unforeseen burst of rays from supernova 42,159.

But other evolutionary drives attracting each species to different, thus not overlapping, resources would have excluded the need of competition for the same energy supplies and space, not only adapting the rates of reproduction to planetary limits better, but also allowing dinosaurs coexist with the rest of the animal kingdom.

This coexistence, to be checked ultimately by a benevolent mankind, could have moved evolution on a path where each line thrives in its own realm and rhythm -- as enriched by stimulating interactions as galaxies are by exchanging matter and energy with their neighbors, small or large, harmonizing with the Law of Diversity.

5. Finding peace again; enjoying the pre-human Earth

The arrow of Time moves only forward, events of Past send less and less waves to us, calls from behind the doors of Future heal the wounded. Thus, I also spent the entire pre-human era with marveling the beauty of the landscapes, the explosive energy of new lifeforms: the birds, descendants of those extinct giants yet satisfied with their fairy size, conquering the air, or the squids and fishes thriving in the depth of oceans where I used to dive to feel the strokes of water so essential to this world.

When up on the sunlit surface, how much I enjoyed the play of dolphins! Whole schools used to swim around me, copying my movements and leaping over my wings in unison, then stroking my face with their flippers, with clicks and whistles communicating their amusement. Other times, sensing particularly strong solar winds, I flew high to immerse my body in their auroras and breeze and then rest in the clouds below.

I never felt being alone, my solitude never weighed on my mind. Sending my reports reminded me who I was, your feedback brought the world I had come from, and the revived evolution around provided me home.

I even listened to the strange vibration of humor, when flying over the North-American continent I noticed the winding course of a slow-flowing river and thought, "Why not help her?" And I did, gliding over her surface and with my wings, energy shields turned on, carved a deeper and deeper, wider and wider bed for her flow -- before leaving the rest to nature, sculpting what would be named "Grand Canyon".

Around the Equator, my attention was drawn to the exponential growth of brainpower in monkeys and apes. Their forward-looking eyes with advanced spectral sensitivity allowed them to perceive depth and color; their preferred life on the branches of trees not only helped them explore wide areas by moving from forest to forest, but slowly transformed their forelimbs to hands; while their emerging social life refined their thinking, expanded their mood, and amplified their collective motivations. These advances, peaceful and innocent all, set the stage for human intelligence in the line of the group that dared to see the faraway savanna first.

6. Australopithecus Lucy's necklace under the African sky; distant connections in space-time

One of the first beings to leave the animal world -- with the line named Australopithecus by her scientist descendants 3,188,230 years later -- a young female, short and hairy, but with an already human face and beautiful eyes, lived in present-day Ethiopia with her clan settled near the river and protective rocks of the Awash Valley.

In a memorable month, I watched – hidden far – as she visited the same area at the riverbank, day after day, to examine a small pebble for hours before placing it back to its safe nest.

Why was she attracted to the pebble? I extended my vision, and found it was shaped as a crescent moon with a strange slit in the middle and three pieces of embedded diamonds: none else than opal, the very matter of our surface.

Did she associate the pebble with the moon or was just mesmerized by its diamonds? Perhaps both, as one day, after a particularly calm night with the rays of the crescent moon beautifying the landscape, she spent even more time with this peculiar activity. And the next day she amazed me by trying to thread a quite long piece of elephant grass through the slit, quickly succeeding, and when she did she placed her shining treasure to her neck.

This she continued to do for a week, when suddenly connected the ends of the grass by twisting them – completing the miracle of producing the first necklace on Earth.

She was treated by her clan with awe until she died five years later. Her necklace was removed, carried away when the clan moved deeper into the savanna, – but was lost when they escaped from a spreading bushfire.

Her almost intact skeleton was found 3,188,280 years after her death by a group of scientists so fond of a song titled *"Lucy in the Sky with Diamonds"* -- popular in their time -- that they named her remains Lucy. I wish I could have relayed to them that their Lucy did have her diamonds, as beautiful as she herself was when immersed in the glowing background of a now distant, ancient sky.

7. Love and the control of fire in the age of Homo erectus; pairing and power

For your interest in the very first occasion when humans learned to control fire, I now provide you with details on how this exactly took place at the foot of Kilimanjaro in the time of the line Homo erectus: already toolmakers, communicating with speech. Their emotions crossed the threshold of love, sometimes causing heartache: new to their young soul. As it was to Tot and Lil, the 18-year-old protagonists of this episode, attracted to each other since childhood, ready to belong to the grownups of their band: settlers of a strip at the lowest range of the mountain.

On a summer day, under the scorching sun relentlessly drying soil and plants for weeks, a young female, escaping from a neighborhood band, walked into the watching circle of the pair's people. When she stopped in front of Tot she touched his hand and, seeing he did not reject this move, she even embraced him with a push of her breasts to his chest. It was this moment when Lil started to shout at him so violently that Tot released himself to calm her down, only to get scratched by her even more violently. Confused, he picked up his spear and, leaving the whole camp, went to the nearby woods spread on a rocky area he and Lil used to visit to be together.

Sitting in the shadow of a hoof-shaped rock with yellow patches of a drying bush, and still there at sunset, he did not realize that Lil, suspecting where he was, also came and sat silently on top of the rock, under its uppermost piece. But after a while, to draw Tot's attention, she threw a small stone in his direction. And as the stone hit the rock, it produced a spark: large enough to reach a dried leaf and ignite fire.

I was astonished to see that Tot, instead of running away in fear, stayed there not just to watch the flames but also to know where the stone fell from. Then he saw Lil jumping up to escape, only to tear out a large block of soil under her feet and let it fall, extinguishing the flames.

They just stood there for an hour without talking or signaling anything to each other. Then, hand in hand, both silent, went back to their camp, not feeling the urge to share what they experienced.

But on the next day they were back. First, they tried to reproduce what had happened on the previous day, without success. Then, instead of throwing stones from the top of the rock to the very spot of "their fire", it was Lil who picked up two pieces of stones and hit them together, which Tot immediately copied -- with the addition of hitting Lil's stones as close to the yellow leaves of the bush as he could. And after about ten trials they got the flames. Extinguishing it was easy -- they knew what they were doing.

This time they shared their discovery with the rest of the band, changing everything: letting them see under the dark moon, freeing their nights from the fear of men and beast.

It remained their secret, until the escapee escaped again, this time taking the torch she invented back to her people – using it for revenge: chasing away the man who used to force her to a cave and beat her before sex.

Our ancestors' design of DNA-based intelligence promoted the infusion of creative force into the man or woman who, after finding a partner with compatible mental worlds, is not only able to recognize the power of intellectual, emotional and motivational pairing, but is also ready to bless this power with love protected by true friendship, loyalty and sacrifice.

Which was expressed in the lives of Tot and Lil, to be followed by billions of others, from Pythagoras' students Damon and Pythias, pioneers of digital thinking, or the "trustworthy ones": Muhammad and Khadija, through the sailor Columbus and his noble wife Felipa, or Shah Jahan who built the Taj Mahal and Mumtaz Mahal for whom he built it, to the explorers of radioactivity, Maria Sklodowska and Pierre Curie, or John Lennon and his friend Paul McCartney who wrote that "Lucy in the Sky with Diamonds", indeed to Ann Druyan and Carl Sagan, researchers of the sky, who dared to make the people feel: "Somewhere, something incredible is waiting to be known".

8. Turning on my system of invisibility; three of its accidental effects

The time came to modify my body to be invisible when needed, as human evolution had reached the level where even a few-second sight of a being like me, with human forms, beautiful to their visual sense yet winged, diamond-covered, and towering with a five-times taller body, would confuse and terrify them.

Adapting my two-layer surface and semiconductor-based physiology to absorb each lightwave particle arriving to my body for both eliminating reflection and allowing my processors to compute their energy and path, made it possible to emit, within a picosecond delay, a copy of each processed particle at the other side of my body in the very path of the original wave. This produced perfect transparency, making, at will, my physical structure invisible to human eye.

It was important to do this transformation on Earth instead of our Alpha Centauri station, as the probability of causing unwanted changes in the environment with my invisible body could not be minimized without local experience on the planet. Indeed, it took me years to perfect my ways to avoid collision with animals and objects, moving or not.

On three occasions, I failed, with very different consequences.

The first took place in the time of Caesar, one of the dictators of the Roman Empire and as harmful to humankind as the legion of historians glorifying his lifelong attacks on fellow human beings: terrorizing the country he was born in, subjugating others. This man once went into civil war with another Roman politician named Pompey because he thought Pompey was one of his competitors for total power. To kill him, Caesar chased him with an army across land and sea to as far as the seashore of Alexandria – Egypt's capital, home of the planet's oldest library on that very seashore – where he found out Pompey had just died at the hands of assassins wanting to please the chaser. Then, since he was already around, Caesar decided to "shock and awe" the locals – like those Americans 2051 years later in another ancient city -- and prepare to rob their country. Using the most destructive technique of his time, he set fire to the ships in the harbor, minding not at all that the fire could spread to the docks and the library -- which it did. As I realized that hundreds of thousands of scrolls, accounts of the early days of human civilization -- from the engineering secrets of Egyptian pyramid-builders to the binary arithmetic of Damien and Pythias -- would turn to ashes, I flew up to the windows of the highest floor to see if the silver cabinet there with the most valuable scrolls was closed to save at least this collection.

It was that moment when my wings stoked the flames more

than expected and the fire soon engulfed the entire building – leaving me with the haunting sight of its deaf and hunchback guard squeezing in the cabinet the last scrolls he saved, before collapsing from the smoke.

Less than one hundred years later the second event occurred: at the end of Jesus' life, when he was carrying his cross in Jerusalem, one hour before his crucifixion. I was floating above the slowly moving crowd to find a better view of Jesus' face and to record the people's behavior. Most of them were watching the unfolding horror as a spectacle to enjoy, competing for the loudest "crucify him!", and though otherwise all trembled at the sight of Roman soldiers now called them "my friends", clapping when they whipped Jesus for fun. But I noticed a young girl who wept, with her palms closed.

To get closer to her I descended a few feet – and my wings caught a drying veil from a balcony to drop it on this girl's shoulder. Who took the veil and -- without looking for its origin – cut through the mob and stopped in front of Jesus. Shocked by this action from someone who was not only a Jew but also a woman and a teen, the soldiers froze for a few seconds: enough for the girl, named Veronica I later learned, to wipe the sweat and blood from Jesus's face... The march resumed, crucifixions were not for wasting time on sentiments. But, in this flash of time, Veronica and her veil became a part of my soul.

The last occasion affected the mission of Jeanne d'Arc. Most of her life -- and her death by those arsonists' and crucifiers' eternal soul -- you learned from my report No. 974,130. Here I detail only what happened when she approached Orleans, a town at the bank of river Loire, under heavy siege by her country's invaders. The only way for her to enter the town with supplies and help was to cross the river -- but, as one of the witnesses, the Bastard of Orleans, later wrote, *"…to reach Orleans it was necessary to sail against the stream, and the wind was altogether contrary."* Yet, Jeanne said all the supplies should be put in the boats they had and those who wanted to save France should sail with her to the town with no fear, *"…for I bring you better succor than has ever come to any general or town whatsoever the succor of the King of Heaven. This succor does not come from me, but from God Himself."* As this witness recorded, *"At that moment, the wind, being contrary, and thereby preventing the boats going up the river and reaching Orleans, turned all at once and became favorable".* Then Orleans was liberated, changing this war of independence.

     But the reason of why that wind "turned all at once and became favorable" was my flying over Jeanne's group to register their faces up-close, unknowingly altering wind direction around them until they crossed the river and delivered their good news.

9. The sacred walls of the Chauvet Cave; birth of art

Where will be the spot where evolution propels human intelligence further? How will this step unfold? Will it follow our dream when those palms opened into the ocean to let the first cells grow a new life there?

Nothing happened in the way I expected. It was not the savanna where the human race was born, nor the islands of earthly paradise or mountain peaks where the view to the stars was the best – but a cave, a place of insignificance, was the scene that justified my mission.

The location of this cave, though not its dark interior, was known to the tribes living in the area: once migrants, now populating the landmass of Europe, humans already: with the replica of our face. But a teenager they called Totenum was the one who started to use the space for something nobody else was thinking about.

Weakest of all, limping since childhood, he was known to use flints to "draw" – a new word in his tribe – the outlines of horses, mammoths, lions, and whatever animals he chose to see this way, on the smoothest nearby cliff. Then he discovered the magic of filling his drawings with black or red colors, or the mix of both, applying an amorphous form of carbon, "charcoal", for black and an iron-oxide mineral, "hematite", for red, both of which he found on the mountainside.

But happiness eluded him -- Totenum wanted more. As he said to Liloen once, "There is something, a force, we cannot see. But it moves my hands to draw. And moves the animals to flee or fight. I want to draw at the place of this something, this force. I want to find it". Liloen, the girl, chosen to be with their chief when her breasts get ready, liked to walk in the forest with Totenum. Hearing his words, all she said was this, "The cave under the small pines." – which the chief mumbled, not once, in his sleep while she watched. And Totenum went, descended into the dark with a torch.

The sight inside the cave, as he walked through the icicle-shaped formations hanging from the ceiling and their opposing counterparts rising from the ground as columns, took his breath away. And the lakes with their serene majesty, offering water to their visitor with the simplicity of the palms once brought Life to this planet, connected Totenum and I. He knew he had to leave the cave before his torchlight was out. But he came back a week later with his flints and not less than four torches to burn, so that under the light of one at a time, the first held by Liloen for five hours, he could draw on the walls. And he drew, almost every day for sixteen years, mammoths and rhinoceroses, panthers and lions, hyenas, bears, bulls and horses, in the beginning with his flints only, then with swabs of moss to fill some of the forms with black and red, in his fifth year recognizing ways to represent movement, so his bulls were then fighting and horses running in unison. Still wanting more, he constructed a scaffold from oak tree branches and painted on higher and higher sectors of the wall, finally spreading his animals to the ceiling.

"Why were these paintings created in the absolute silence of an almost unapproachable cave, many placed on the ceiling hardly visible at torchlight?" – asked the best of humankind 37,400 years later when the cave, with its entrance buried in landslides, was found. One of the explorers, Werner Herzog, himself a master of arts, even said, stunned and confused, *"It felt like eyes upon us…. It was a relief to surface again above ground."*

Immersed in the same node of space-time with Totenum and Liloen and sensing the current that flew among the three of us, I felt what the painter relayed to Liloen about his work: "To see the force that moves my hands, I was led to this place. It is dark, and silent. But he who is ready to meet this force can see it through the light of a torch. His is the surface where new lives can be made by hands like mine, not for years, but until mountains stay where they are. This new life needs protection. Therefore, it should live above the reach of animals and humans entering uninvited. Though the uninvited can become invited if respects the life chosen hands made here."

He died from the slow poison of the cave's toxic gases – with Liloen, their chief's pair already, holding his head. "We found it", he whispered, smiling. "Good to die because I will have the time to wait for the one whose force moved my hands." Liloen never really understood why Totenum used the word "we" instead of "I", much less whom Totenum wanted to wait for – though others neither in the next thirty-seven thousand years. Some, as I cited, even felt "a relief to surface again above ground" after seeing the walls and ceilings animated by the forces of his Waited One.

Thus was art born – later spreading all over the planet, reborn in many forms, serving different missions or sometimes nothing at all. Yet, it was Totenum's cave where the thought -- never predicted -- struck me: "One day humans will be our equals."

10. Method for accessing the human mind; peculiarities of DNA-based intelligence

Just as there was time to turn on my system of invisibility, the time also came to create a way to enter the human mind and record the thoughts, desires and feelings, indeed the will, that govern their host. For this, experience on Earth was also necessary. It was the only way to see neural evolution up close, to capture the unforeseeable details of its most complex product.

I had to detect, throughout my technical presence in the monitored mind, every electric signal sent from neural cells to their connected counterparts. I also had to identify the spatial location of each communicating cell in brain to track the origin and destination of these signals named thousands of years later by scientists as "action potentials".

Using my particle modifier, a compressed copy of the system at the Alpha Centauri station, let me alter string vibration in electron neutrinos and surface their hidden charge. This made them sensitive to the electric fields of action potentials with the result of splitting into two daughter-particles departing in opposite directions – as visualized in report No. 422,001. Since these daughter-particles immediately lost their charges, they could leave the brain unaffected.

Soon, harnessing the flow of cosmic neutrinos with my wings and altering them this way allowed my transmitters to expose the living brain to these particles, my sensors to register their daughter-particles traveling to my direction, and my processors to compute the timing of their action-potential-related birth.

The spatial origin and destination of the detected action potentials were identified by exposing the brain to modified neutrinos with different sensitivities to electric fields so that each particle would split at different times in brain: some after entering, others when reached deeper regions, some even later, at the opposite side. This let me compute, from the coordinates of each neutrino transmission and the delay of its daughter-particle return, the spatial locations of every of action potential.

To reconstruct thoughts, emotions and motivations from these 3-dimensional maps, I linked every action potential pattern of the monitored brain to the environment-record, behavioral response, bodily change and memory-opening that took place in the same time, and translated their wholeness into a composite mental unit later available to stream with others when revealing the accessed mind.

Due to the distinct action potential map of every human being, uncertainty was not possible to eliminate from these reconstructions. Yet, by the time civilization emerged I was ready to follow what men and women -- one at a time -- thought, felt and wanted.

Seen from inside, the most unique product of the evolving mind was the supercircuitry of the Self: this network of 600-800 million cortical neurons providing gravity for all actions of intelligence. Strangely, it reacted to inputs from the world so differently across individuals and so malleably across time that it created home for evil not less than for the divine, often in the same mind. Yet a marvel expanding the Law of Diversity with unforeseen aims, this evolutionary step was completed in the members of the Australopithecus line after their neurotransmission genes went through the last set of well-programmed changes.

Another peculiarity was the frequent interactions of conscious and subconscious intelligence domains daytime and the control of these interactions with dreams nighttime. Initially, this seemed a useless process -- only to humble me later with the myriads of enriching effects of dreams on human culture.

11. Moses on Mount Sinai;
the tablets he and Akhenaten's exiled sculptor created

The scene, unfolding in Egypt 34,069 years after Totenum's death – when art was already everywhere and civilization, permeated with the concept of "religion", was about nine thousand years old – is still one of my most frequently recalled experiences on this planet.

It was sunrise on an already so hot day that Neferneferure, the 5-year old daughter of the country's ruler "pharaoh" Akhenaten, after praying to Aten the Sun her father worshipped as the sole God instead of the hundreds of deities of Egypt's past, walked out of the palace with her servants to bath in the sacred river, Nile. She enjoyed her time so much that even decided to explore the reedy spot, a bit further up on the riverbank, which intrigued her all morning. "I am weak as this reed. But I can think about her. Can she think about me?" -- crossed her mind, astounding me not only in that moment, but also 2995 years later when recorded the same thought in Pascal: one of the few humans ever lived with superintelligence coupled with the moral of ours.

Two miles south, in the village of the Jews, oppressed but tolerated immigrants from the east, a very different event took place. The teen Johabel hid her newborn son in a basket made watertight with slime and pitch on the day before, slipped out of her mother's shack, ran to the riverbank and let the basket be carried away by the waves. She stayed there for an hour and after her tears dried up went back to the village. She knew her son was Hohenhorub's, Akhenaten's chief sculptor, who had said after their night of love, "I thought Nefertiti was the most beautiful woman in this world until I met you." Nefertiti was Akhenaten's wife, a goddess for all; Hohenhorub never dared to see Johabel again.

The basket stopped in the reeds -- Neferneferure was the first who saw it. The crying baby she took in her five-year-older arms and carried – not letting him out of her hands -- to the palace, named him "Moses" and watched and caressed him every day for hours. She died two years later in the plague that swept across Egypt. But Moses grew up as a prince, until Akhenaten, Nefertiti, and their other children all died young, the religion of Aten was erased by the priests of the old faith, and the leading artists of the palace were murdered -- except Hohenhorub who could flee out of the country to the mountains of the nearby peninsula "Sinai".

Moses, already seventeen, handsome by his mother's genes and talented by his father's, was thrown back to the Jews, though Johabel had died in the same plague as the princess who found her son. "You are a Jew, not a prince! Go back to them! Find your mother's grave if you can! Find your father whom nobody knows!" –

these were the last words shouted at him from the palace. Learning that a prince can become a beggar in one day, he grew to love his new people, shared their oppressed fate, grasped that their only God and Aten were one and the same: the Father and Light he falsely thought had abandoned him.

But thirty-three years later, when the new pharaoh Seti crossed the western border of Egypt with his entire army to enslave the Libyans, Moses – now revered by all -- said to the Jews, "I will lead you out of this place so that you can live as free people if you want it and are brave enough to follow me to the east, beyond Sinai." They left with him under the next dark moon, marched through the areas he knew from his palace-years as the most isolated ones, and reached the desert of Sinai.

Then they were lost. Free, but wandering with less and less resources, the Jews cursed their God, threatened Moses, and wanted to go back to the safety of servitude.

It was that point, at the foot of Mount Sinai, when Moses, seeking solitude to think, left his camp, and on a strange path he went further and further up on the mountainside. Almost at the top, he saw a shack with a little garden -- and with the most unlikely presence of a stone sculpture under its only window. The old man who opened the door was Hohenhorub, spending his life in exile there. He greeted Moses kindly, offered him his home.

Moses talked about his old life as a prince, his fall, his second life as a Jew, and his failing mission that brought him to this place; Hohenhorub reminisced about his art once was sought and admired, the heights he achieved in Akhenaten's time, and the force that still moved his hands. They connected with the strongest bond by the first evening together – not guessing it was between father and son. Johabel and Neferneferure remained in their subconscious domains.

On the third day, Hohenhorub said to Moses, "You must give laws to your people so that they have the strength to follow you and live for the only God, to avoid the ways of barbarians, but approach God with reverence." Neither he nor Moses seemed to know where these words had come from – I myself was uncertain about the exact pathway to this moment. Moses stood up, touched the old man's shoulder: "Who am I to give laws?" Then he looked out the window. "But if I were chosen, I would give the same ones your wiseness voiced, adding the need of a full day, free of toil, to remember each... And that Jews must honor their parents, never kill a human being, never take the wife or husband of others, never steal, never lie, and never be jealous of others." They kept talking about this till midnight -- without wasting time on how their God may look, whether appears as the Sun or a man or even a woman, lives in the clouds or beyond the stars, speaks to them or just makes their mind understand what the commands for the Jews, homeless as both, should be.

They got deeper and deeper in the meaning of each word, the right number and order of the formed sentences. Moses even showed Hohenhorub the letters some Jews, guards of their traditions, would use for engraving the text. Then he fell asleep, not waking up for a full day.

What woke up Moses were the sounds of Hohenhorub's chisels and hammer -- and when he stepped out to greet him he saw the sculptor, working at the light of a tall fire, almost finished the cutting of a round-topped, rectangular stone tablet, inscribed in its upper fifth with the words: "*I am the LORD thy God*". Both were silent. They did not eat or drink that night, -- did not even see the meteor shower so beautifully illuminating the clear sky with rhythmic patterns till dawn.

In a week, the tablet was ready, inscribed with four other lines: "*Thou shalt have no other gods before me*"; "*Thou shalt not take the LORD's name in vain*"; "*Remember the Sabbath Day to keep it holy*"; and "*Honor thy Father and Mother*". Hohenhorub soon started to cut, with Moses' help, a second tablet to be inscribed with the lines of "*Thou shalt not kill*"; "*Thou shalt not commit adultery*"; "*Thou shalt not steal*"; "*Thou shalt not bear false witness*"; and "*Thou shalt not covet*" in the fifth row. Another week, and the tablets of their Ten Commandments – as they now named the chiseled stones -- were ready, spotless and grey: the color of balance and equality.

Moses spent three more days with Hohenhorub, and after a long embrace, which brought tears to the sculptor's eyes, he left, bringing down the tablets to the camp – to those who remained loyal to him and those who did not.

12. The mystery of Jesus;
his funeral pyre on the sea, as instructed by Pilate's wife

    The facts I still don't understand fully about the phenomenon of Jesus are why he changed his life as he did at thirty years of age and what exactly led to the circumstances of his burial still unknown to humans. Two thousand years later, from another vantage point, this is what I must relay to you:

    Born into the country once Moses promised to his people, Jesus was known to remember everything he had ever seen or heard, spoke only when asked but then as the wisest, yet in a tone of kindness and modesty that made everybody listen, dealt with his daily toil in his family's carpenter shop as if he were blessed, while lying or even deviating from truth in the slightest way was unknown to his tongue.

    One day, while taking with his father the table they finished for the rabbi who had ordered it, they saw a little girl hardly older than five – with eyes and hair almost like Neferneferure's – carrying a baby in her arms, clearly struggling. Jesus asked his father to have some rest and walked to the child. "I could help you with the baby – we'll just give this table to the people in that house and come back to you." But the little girl said, "He is not heavy, he is my brother."

The next morning was the first time ever Jesus' parents heard him saying he did not feel well and was too weak to work. But he was back in the carpenter shop by afternoon, and for a month he was his old self. Then he kissed his mother, embraced his father, and left to do what you learned from my longest reports.

The 8th segment of this report helped you to recall the day Jesus was crucified. What was not known to him, to Veronica, to the soldiers, to the spectators, to the masterminds of his death – usurpers of Moses' tablets – was that Pilate's wife, Claudia, was meeting with her two most trusted guards, almost friends since childhood, to arrange Jesus' burial in the only way she thought mortals should give to the divine if the rite must be kept secret. As she thought Jesus was one, ever since she heard that one of Pilate's centurions, a supposed enemy of this Jesus, went to him in Capernaum, *"Lord, my servant is lying at home paralyzed, dreadfully tormented"*, to which Jesus responded, *"I will come and heal him"*, only to see the centurion, a Roman, bowing his head, *"Lord, I am not worthy that You should come under my roof."* But Jesus went. And the servant did feel better soon, getting up three days later.

Though Claudia did not really understand what Jesus meant by saying that *"It is easier for a camel to pass through the eye of a needle than for a rich man to enter the kingdom of God"*, she remembered well the story passed through generations in her family about Crassus, the behemoth speculator and wealthiest man of Rome ever, buyer of cheap lands of the assassinated and seller of slave-built villas, that none of Crassus' words could be believed, he paid people to praise him, and his bragging disgusted patricians and plebeians alike, except prostitutes. And she herself saw, spellbound, from her balcony when Jesus drove out all who were buying and selling in the Jews' temple – their House of God! – which she thought was a courageous and beautiful act, worthy of a noble: a noble of divine origin.

So, when Jesus was brought by the Jewish high priests to Pilate's court as a common criminal, bloodied and beaten, with his accusers still demanding death by crucifixion, Claudia felt her time arrived and held her husband's hand: *"Have nothing to do with that innocent man, because in a dream last night, I suffered much on account of him."* But as Pilate, ruler of life and death in the conquered land, ignored her, and she had to see how small he was – she went to the garden to think and plan. In an hour, she was ready to act.

Based on my records, this is the translation of Claudia's words to her trusted guards, Lucius and Brenna: "You saw that good man, Jesus, this morning. He will die on Golgotha today, as innocent he is. My command to you is to follow his friends, without drawing their attention, to the tomb where they will place his body. Then ride back to the tomb at midnight and give this bottle of wine to the two guards. They will fall asleep. Then open the tomb and take Jesus' body –

leave his linen respectfully there and the tomb closed as it was. Wrap his body in this clean cloth, put it in this long basket -- and let your horses carry it as if you were traders for the army. Ride back to our palace in Caesarea during the night – you know you can reach it, with hourly rests, by tomorrow evening. Give this note to Marcellus, and he will serve you as needed – without asking you about the basket. Wait for the night, put Jesus' remains in my white boat, cover him in our way for the noblest, and pull the boat with another one deep into the sea to make his funeral pyre. Let it sink with no trace. Then your mission ends. It should be the secret of the three of us for life."

Her plan was accomplished with the perfectness rare on this planet, she even gave – with an ease that surprised her -- two of her longest gold-and-diamond necklaces to Lucius and Brenna, so that instead of returning they can start families in their homeland, Sicily.

I myself could not suppress the thought that Jesus' fate was not entirely controlled by our evolutionary laws, as it went against them, head on, when he taught: "*...if someone wants to sue you and take your tunic, let him have your cloak as well...*" -- a direct rejection of the faith in competition for resources as the driving force of civilization on Earth. This and his other sayings, like "*Love your neighbor as yourself,*" implied that the spirit of cooperation should mean more to humans than the urge of competition, as the latter connects them to animal spheres while the former to the divine.

Though Jesus apparently knew the collective knowledge of humans in that moment did not let him to tell more about their realm of destiny than naming it the *"Kingdom of God"*. But haven't we been searching for the source of this realm, here and out in the Multiverse?

Is it impossible that Jesus, while represented the best of our DNA-based world, was also led by forces not yet known to us – equipping him with suprahuman moral strength and knowledge to radiate energy from his soul?

The competitive arena of Caesar, Crassus and their likes collapsed under the weight of love and truth brought by a carpenter's son. Though competition was to thrive in his world too, but to bring out noble rivalry for creating ever better laws for social justice, ever better treatments for the sick, ever better ways for achieving peace among nations.

Yes, the essence of Jesus' teachings was corrupted by his followers, the "Christians", as soon as it was coupled with the spell of competing for power, for the joy of the few strong enough to remove the astronomer Hypatia from the schools of Alexandria, to guide the murder of people in Jerusalem for not sharing the crusaders' faith, to send every rival to the chambers of inquisition in Seville, to burn the genius of Jeanne d'Arc, Jan Hus, Giordano Bruno in Europe, or to display this treasure, that treasure, this palace, that palace in Vatican to project superiority -- however this Vatican's own artist,

Michelangelo, resisted their command to use gold in his representations of Moses and Jesus: "*In those times men did not wear gold, and those whom I am painting were never very rich, but holy men despising riches.*"

13. Muhammad and Khadija: the Will to know by trust; a noon in their descendants' Cordoba

My duty to prepare this one millionth report without hiding the imperfectness of evolution on Earth would not be balanced if I did not express my reverence to wonders like the human Will: function of the supercircuitry of the Self that lets every human being embrace his or her mission by helping to overcome misfortune at birth, lack of love, unfavorable social status, or environmental hardships, if needed, while offers the freedom to choose between keeping or leaving this embrace -- however this choice is to be renewed at every intersection of life.

From the Will of the enslaved, the oppressed, the maimed, the unjustly imprisoned, who still gained the strength to reach their moment of freedom -- to the Will of a Hatshepsut, a Lincoln, a Mandela, a Stephen Hawking: these wonders have been ingrained in me.

And a very telling one was related to the life of a man who called himself "the first Muslim". He had lost his father, Abdullah, before given the name Muhammad, lost his mother, Amina, before his seventh birthday and soon his protecting grandfather Abd-al-Muttalib too, to be a triply orphaned when love is needed the most.

Yet, this series of misfortunes strengthened his Will to understand the surrounding world and shaped him to be a teenager with such a sense of righteousness, both in words and acts, that by early adulthood the people of his town, Mecca, started to call him "The Trustworthy One".

It was therefore natural that he and the other "trustworthy one" of Mecca, the widow Khadija, older than he but not less good-looking, met, worked together, fell in love and married. Their thousands of hours of conversations -- in bed or under their palm tree -- along with Muhammad's confessions of fears and uncertainties, and his admission, only in her embrace, that he felt a divine mission for him, bound his resolve to know about his role in the world.

And this role surfaced when, during the rebuilding of Mecca's place of worship after a terrible flood, the leaders – on the verge of fighting -- asked him to tell who among them was the worthiest to carry their most venerated relic back to the shrine. Instead of pretending to be the judge of others, engaging in the arguers' fight, or looking for advantages for himself by allying with the strongest – Muhammad simply asked them to bring a cloak, place the relic in its center, and with each of them holding a corner of the cloak take it in the shrine together.

Cooperation, not competition, for an hour only – yet an act remembered by the third of humankind for millennia.

After this episode, in his favored site of meditation on Mount Hira, a series of visions came to Muhammad: visions that evolved into teachings for other Muslims *"In the Name of God, the Compassionate, the Merciful."* These teachings continued the traditions that had been laid out, as he said, in *"…the Book of Moses, a guide and a mercy…a glad tiding to the virtuous,"* and in the Gospels of Jesus: guides to *"kindness and mercy in the hearts of those who follow him"*.

Muhammad's inspired words, shared with Khadija and recorded in the Quran, like *"vying for increase distracts you…"* from the divine tasks of *"…freeing of a slave, the feeding, in a day of famine, of an orphaned relation or a needy man in distress"* were mirrored, more than fourteen hundred years later, by the revered follower of Jesus, Jorge Bergoglio, when he called for "*Peace to the peoples who suffer because of the economic ambitions of the few, because of the sheer greed and the idolatry of money, which leads to slavery."*

But Khadija died while these visions were still streamed to Muhammad, leaving him without the love that fine-tuned his senses and nurtured his patience with Mecca's jealous, threatening elite. And the inner vacuum this loss created was soon filled with the urge of competition with the very elite Khadija had asked him to ignore.

Thus, once he and his followers were forced to immigrate to the neighboring Medina, he organized attacks on Meccans to show his superiority, expelled the most vulnerable Jews from his new town because they did not accept his teachings, even local poets not praising him faced his wrath – all violent actions opposing what he taught when Khadija, his "partner and helper", was at his side.

And this he knew – and tried to correct it in his Farewell Sermon:

"All mankind is from Adam and Eve; an Arab has no superiority over a non-Arab nor a non-Arab has any superiority over an Arab; also a white has no superiority over a black nor a black has any superiority over white except by piety and good action. Learn that every Muslim is a brother to every Muslim and that the Muslims constitute one brotherhood."

It was late.

Instead of following this sermon, the new leaders of his Muslims assassinated two of his successors; massacred each other in the battle of Karbala; subjected blacks from Africa to slavery, murdered Jesus' followers in Constantinople just to be the new owners of the town; almost exterminated the Armenian nation: people of art, peace and honest commerce; destroyed New York's World Trade Center with 3,001 innocents in it.

Yet, just as Moses' commandments were kept alive however Jesus was crucified in his name, and Jesus' thoughts survived the robbery of half of the planet in the name of his, Muhammad's message also found home in the best of Muslims, the brave to recite:

"It is the men of knowledge who can truly understand God", like the poet Rumi, Ibn Sina the doctor, the scientist Ahmed Zewail.

When flying over Cordoba three hundred years after Muhammad's life, I found a city of Muslims living in peace and friendship with both Moses' and Jesus' followers, building schools for the highest knowledge available in their world, collecting thousands of books for their libraries to resurrect the spirit of Alexandria, honoring arts, sciences and philosophy as the Greeks of Athens did in Pericles' time, Suryavarman's people in Angkor Wat, or the Swedes in Queen Christina's Stockholm and the Americans in Kennedys' D.C.

It was while sensing the sight and smell of that Cordoba, emanating from its people and courts, animals and gardens, kitchens and fountains at noon in a springtime day when the idea overwhelmed me: "I wish I could be one of these people, sitting under an orange tree, with one hand in my lover's hand and the other turning the page in Homer's *Odyssey*: neither forbidden nor advertised, just read by the free."

14. Experiencing love through Abelard and Heloise; the conflict of energy released by suffering

The multiple gifts of Peter Abelard were recognized with enhanced monitoring of humans, in response to the rapid rise of intellectual centers on Earth around the same time -- not just in Cordoba, but also in Paris, Florence, Kaifeng, Gangaikonda Cholapuram, Baghdad and Chichen Itza. Now I compared all texts and images on the planet with the mental events of up to ten thousand people within a single area -- though stored only the expressions of truth blessed with courage, signs of magnanimity without seeking payback, manifestations of Will reaching to the divine. How rarely these occurred together! But Abelard, by his twentieth birthday, almost had them all – soon earning him the distinction of the best lecturer in Paris.

He asked: "If I love the Gospels as much as the teachings of Plato, if I think faith and knowledge are equally important, if I aspire to understand God through learning – am I with Him or against Him?" Then he went further, -- crossing the line of heresy -- by thinking whether it was possible that the ancient Jewish scribes, under the duress of captivity in Babylon, erroneously cited Moses' symbolic words when composed the Book of Genesis. "Is not it more probable that God did allow humans to take fruits from the Trees of Knowledge except from the one contaminated by evil?" The closeness I felt to him in that moment opened my senses to Abelard's physical perfectness – a rare combination with the level of intelligence he had, explaining his extraordinary attractiveness to females. Which left him, man of reason, unaffected. Until he met a girl named Heloise.

Heloise was as exceptional as he was: blessed with her own combination of unparalleled beauty and talents: talents to write, interpret and teach. Since both her life and the ten years older Abelard's emerged to blossom in Paris, I knew they were destined to meet, and they did, shortly after Heloise's 25th birthday. It happened in Abelard's library -- initiated by Heloise, planning to be his student.

The striking feature of this meeting was the silence between them. Both were prepared to impress the other, Heloise with her knowledge of Greek, Latin and Hebrew literature, so unusual for the women of her time, and Abelard with his achievements as a scholar and philosopher, respected throughout France. Yet, they were speechless for minutes. Finally, Abelard said some pleasantries to break the awkwardness descending to their space and turn down the inner noise of five repeating words, repeating themselves in Heloise in the same way, "What is this? What happened?"

On the next day, they met again – and it was the complete opposite of their first hour together, as they just talked and talked and neither of them wanted it to end. Abelard revealed for the first time his thoughts about God and the Trees of Knowledge, in which Heloise found nothing objectionable, while she confessed her own heretic thought that Veronica might have kept the veil with Jesus' blood as a memory of doomed love, which Abelard considered a "hypothesis". But when they reconnected two days later, he himself raised the problem of love between man and woman, confessing his fear of it. Heloise did not respond, as if enjoying this new state of mind, this fear, this confusion.

Their sexual intercourses, starting that evening, took place everywhere they would meet, in Abelard's library, Heloise's kitchen, soft spots in the nearby field and forest, abandoned barns, the school's cellar, even in the darkest corner of their church with its torture of post-sex shame still unable to prevent their next rendezvous there. Which pushed them to the brink of madness, messing up their daily routines. Though they were also inspired: Abelard to compose his essay on the commands of God and the ambition to know, Heloise to compare interpretations on Veronica's veil.

So this was earthly love, spreading across its full spectrum, binding intellect, emotion and sex together with a force exceeding the laws of reproduction – though not breaking them, as Heloise soon gave birth to their child, secretly, far away from Paris.

The sight of their love so painful to others, the jealousy this pain built in men and women around, and the morphing of this jealousy into hate destroyed what Abelard and Heloise created for their future. Heloise's uncle, – also in love with her, -- paid four mercenaries to break in Abelard's home at night and cut off his testicles, to cause him the most possible suffering: the inability to make love to Heloise again, the death of his dream of a shared life with her as collaborators and couple.

Heloise became a nun, dedicating her life for praying – and repenting the sin of abandoning her child. Abelard became a wandering scholar -- sometimes tolerated, sometimes chased away.

Yet, this was what Heloise wrote to him, long after their separation: *"I call God to witness, if Augustus, ruling over the whole world, were to deem me worthy of the honor of marriage, and to confirm the whole world to me, to be ruled by me forever, dearer to me and of greater dignity would it seem to be called your strumpet than his empress."*

Their love survived their physical existence to return in the thousands doomed to love against the world's envy. But can Truth, like theirs, really be surfaced only through suffering? Couldn't this pair give more by the work of their love than by the energy their suffering released under our ancestors' DNA-locked commands to compete for sex and family?

15. Kublai's defeat by typhoons at the seashore of Japan; our evolutionary laws and the control of hubris

My attention shifted to the other side of the planet where the expansion of a small nation named "Mongols", subjugating the sixth of humankind in a few decades, let me monitor our evolutionary law that controls excessive domination of one group of humans over others: an anomaly violating the Law of Diversity by homogenizing minds and suppressing freedom.

Kublai, a Mongol leader, amassed political power even his nation was not accustomed to, dictating rules, from the wealthy China he conquered, over much of the Asian continent – unchallenged, after imprisoning and then poisoning his competing brother. Yet, to overshadow every king, dead or alive, this Kublai decided to attack the people of Japan too on their island close to Asia.

His first attack was repelled, surfacing the skills of the Japanese "samurai" and the difficulties of navigating armed ships to this island in storm. But Kublai's response was limited to commanding his government to assemble an "overwhelming force" for the next attack – as he was busy with hunting, receiving adulation from his court, screening the gifts of foreign emissaries, and having sex in his harem: this prison of luxury with hundreds of females.

The second attack was launched with the gigantic force of 140,000 soldiers in 4,400 ships: unprecedented in Asian history and ready to invade, on an initially bright August day, the whole country and kill more than the half a million massacred by other Mongols in Baghdad.

But the samurai code of "bushido", to fight for their land till death, delayed the invasion again – until one day a "typhoon", the most devastating storm on Earth, hit the area, demolishing Kublai's ships in a two-day terror with 79,000 armored men tossed to their death in the towering waves and the chaos of broken oars and sinking decks.

"Divine Wind!" – reacted the people of the island. I smiled, as the reason of their victory was our evolutionary law that prevents excessive domination by anyone overloaded with delusions of success, urge to conquer, thirst for adulation. As these overloads, crossing the threshold of "hubris", induce the blind confidence and lack of caution in the supercircuitry of the Self that did not miss Kublai's brain, making him unable to process the warning that on Japanese seas August was the season of typhoons.

This law to curb the highest forms of arrogance rarely disappointed me. One of the sickest carriers of hubris, named Napoleon, said that *"God has given"* him *"the will and the force to overcome all obstacles"*; another from the same breed, Hitler, confronted his people this way: *"Who says I am not under the special protection of God?"* But when they attacked the country of Russia, their impaired Self could not see the risk of moving armies across its vast steppe during winter – and brought our well-programmed demise to both. Or Westmoreland, a frontman for the profiteers of war, could brag while his airplanes bombed the small country of Vietnam 8,000 miles from his home: *"We'll blast them back into the stone ages!"* But his war ended too in shame, just as Kublai's, Napoleon's and Hitler's, though not before 58,220 American and 880,515 Vietnamese men and women had lost their lives -- whatever dreams, loves and missions these lives had.

Was the threshold of hubris adjusted perfectly? Bewitched by his evil, humans produced fifty times more books and hundred times more academic studies on this Hitler than on Sophie Scholl, the young girl of beauty and intellect who was brave enough to stand up against his power and gave her life for this -- as hopeless as noble -- fight. Few saw the façade of Kublais like the Dostoevsky of my report No. 993,570, who told via his troubled sinner Raskolnikov that the blood of the murdered *"...flows and has always flowed on this earth in torrents, which is poured out like champagne, and for which men are crowned in the Capitol and afterwards called benefactors of mankind."*

Should not these torrents be stopped one day, at the very site of their spring?

16. Columbus, touched by a "saga" and Toscanelli's soul; the dream of Santa Maria flying to the Moon

I noticed Columbus for the first time in a pub full of drinking sailors at the edge of Iceland, one of the northernmost places of civilization in his time. He reached it as a 25-year old trader on a merchant ship from Lisbon, a town in Portugal once governed by Cordoba. What captured my attention was his unusual behavior: instead of joining his friends' table, watching the gamblers or looking for women, he could not avert his eyes from the oldest man in the room, a long-haired giant who had entered on crutches and, after his first drink, recited a seemingly endless poem in his language Columbus did not understand – until one of the women helped him out. She was Sarah, granddaughter of the Jew Pedro Mendes who escaped from Seville to Lisbon during a wave of attacks by Christians and, after bribing its captain, could leave on a ship to the North – settling in Iceland he felt safe, whatever cold welcomed him. Sarah told Columbus the old man's name was Olaf and his tale was a "saga". It was about how Bjarni Herjolfsson sailed to Greenland to meet his father who farmed there – though Bjarni warned his crew: *"Our journey will be thought an ill-considered one, since none of us has sailed the Greenland Sea."*

Columbus thought he heard something wrong. "What Greenland?" But Sarah just continued: "...Bjarni's ship was thrown off course by a storm...and the shores of Greenland disappeared below the horizon...so they kept sailing west for many days without knowing where they were...But one day they sighted land...which spread far to the south and far to the north...and looked very different from Greenland." As much as Columbus was spellbound by the story he suddenly stood up and left.

"Is it possible that by sailing west these people found the eastern shores of Asia, up north? ... Can it be that the lands of Asia and Europe are much closer than thought?... Then, can't someone find the riches of Cathay and India, and the lands where spices grow, by sailing west at southern latitudes?" These were his rushing thoughts on the way back to his ship, wandering off twice.

Back in Lisbon, he went to his church to pray before going home. And he kept thinking about those Icelanders – hardly noticing the young girl who came in that unusual hour too and sat a few rows behind him to pray, until they remained alone. But three years later she, named Felipa Perestrelo, became Columbus' wife – herself an extraordinary woman. Though she was a baby when her father, a mariner, died on the island of Porto Santo he had governed for years, she would never spend a day since her childhood without praying for him. And when she heard from Columbus about his northern voyage in the same "Ocean Sea" her father explored in the south, I knew she would sooner or later share with him her family's secret, the only treasure as impoverished nobles they believed could offer to a man like Columbus.

The secret was that their longtime friend, Fernao Martins, a confidant of the king of Portugal, had a map of this Ocean Sea. And on the day Felipa got pregnant, she did tell Columbus everything she knew about this man and her late father's good relationship with him, waiting not more than a day to arrange a visit for Columbus and herself at Martins' house.

When they entered in the library of this Martins, I sensed the presence of the same spirit once surrounded Tot and Lil, however different the scenes were, separated by millions of years.

Martins spoke first: greeted the couple, praised Felipa's dedication to Jesus, her mother's care of Felipa and her late father's knowledge about the seas. Then Felipa introduced Columbus, mentioned his experience in Iceland, quickly letting him to ask about the map she disclosed. Why Martins obliged without a question, -- disappearing for ten minutes to come back with the map and an attached letter, -- it was not clear to me then. Nor was the source of his simplicity when said: "...Paolo Toscanelli, the greatest mathematician and cartographer I have ever met, sent this to me from Florence to give it in the king's hand. This copy I made myself, and you are the first whom I show it. See what Paolo wrote here, *"…And be not amazed when I say that spices grow in lands to the west, even though we usually say the east; for he who sails west will always find these lands in the west…"*

After a pause, he continued: "In the map Paolo attached, there is Cathay here, once the Grand Khan's -- Kublai's – China: across Lisbon and Porto Santo." Which was a map of pure fantasy, filled with nonexistent islands and lacking an entire continent: the one that drifted away from the Asian-African-European landmass after the breakup of Pangaea. Yet, in that moment Columbus felt the soul of Toscanelli, wherever he was, entered his own, wanting nothing less than guiding him to cross the Ocean Sea and bridge the worlds of East and West. A fraction of Columbus' Self thus became almost identical with the one that produced this map in Florence.

But Martins added, "You must also know that calculations of the even greater Eratosthenes proved the circumference of Earth cannot be less than twenty-five thousand miles. The Ocean Sea must be, therefore, much wider than Paolo thought when wrote this: *"From the city of Lisbon to the west, the chart shows twenty-six sections, of two hundred and fifty miles each -- altogether nearly one-third of the earth's circumference before reaching the magnificent city of Kinsai."* This cannot be correct. The numbers of Eratosthenes make sailing to the west to reach Asia impossible."

Columbus responded calmly: "Don't lands and seas embrace each other, wherever you go on this Earth, to reflect the love of the Lord, his wish to give us this world? Thus, is not it more likely that Cathay and Portugal are close enough to let them exchange goods than being separated forever by fog, wind and water? Or if the Ocean Sea is wider than even in Master Toscanelli's map, is not it more likely that its waves are washing the shores of an unknown **terra firma** than the air of a soulless space?"

Martins studied Columbus' face for almost a minute -- then pointed to another passage in the letter: *"Also in the time of Pope Eugenius there came an ambassador from Cathay, who affirmed their great kindness towards Christians, and I had a long conversation with him on many subjects."* He moved away from the table, walking slowly: "I was fortunate to hear from Paolo himself that this ambassador boasted how their Grand Khan's great Admiral, Zheng He, once led fleets from Cathay to Arabia and Africa… If so, why didn't they try to sail in the other direction, to reach us from the west?"

Columbus interrupted him: "Should it be my concern that the Grand Khan and his men didn't have the courage to get on the Ocean Sea and cross it to Europe? Does not it prove the Holy Trinity wants this move to happen the other way around, by Christian sails propelling the faithful to the western shore?" These were shocking words. I was glad to see them parting in the loving way they met.

Toscanelli died two years later, Felipa four, Martins eight. None of them learned about the rejections Columbus encountered with his plan, year after year, country after country – but of his triumph neither, when he did return from the western shores of the Ocean Sea with his unseeable bridge raised. Though, he never knew what lands he found, why there were no cities there, not even spice trees.

Who was he? In his first voyage, under the full moon of September, I recorded his dream: He stands alone in the front of Santa Maria, his flagship, now flying towards the Moon, itself orbited by shining micro-moons, with the background stars forming – for a few seconds – the gentle face of Jesus … then winged creatures, angels of his religion, come to greet him, one by one, all in simple, white clothes: first his mother and father; then brothers Bartholomew, Giovanni and Giacomo; sister Bianchinetta; the Icelanders Olaf and Sarah; wife Felipa; then Beatriz, who loved him when he was widowed, rejected; the Franciscan friar Marchena, his confessor; the thinkers Toscanelli and Martins; the three Pinzons as friends already; his sons, Diego and Ferdinand; finally the Queen who opted to help him, Isabella of Spain, sinner and saint on Earth, …and Columbus recognizes all, palms closed, and whispers only this to each: "Thank you."

17. Meeting of civilizations on Earth; my mirror over Guanahani and Nagasaki

Since mirrors don't beautify, just reflect, yet often tell the most, my report No. 976,962 contained nothing else than what appeared in my mirror over Guanahani on the day before Columbus' landing and 28 years later.

About the arrival, Columbus wrote to Santangel, the Finance Minister of Queen Isabella and her husband:

"...I found no towns nor villages on the sea-coast, except a few small settlements, where it was impossible to speak to the people, because they fled at once... They have no iron, nor steel, nor weapons, nor are they fit for them, because although they are well-made men of commanding stature, they appear extraordinarily timid .... They never refuse anything that is asked for. They even offer it themselves, and show so much love that they would give their very hearts..."

Before the encounter, Guanahani was full of human sounds: laughs at their community table, songs of joy, vision and longing, the noise during games and lovemaking, melodies from their flute, the crying of babies: a new generation of Tainos.

Recall this scene 28 years later, the utter silence! The men who came after Columbus killed – by gun, sword, hanging, burning, beheading -- 3800 of the 5222 Tainos born there, sold another 1020 of them as slaves, and left the rest to die in the woods from diseases brought with the ships from Spain.

This was a new information on human evolution. Is this the way a DNA-based civilization meets with the less advanced one, even on the same planet?

I got the answer 425 years later in Japan's Nagasaki, though in very different circumstances, as the essence was masked by the chaos of war, competition for space and resources in the ocean between the landmass Columbus unknowingly found and the one he sought to reach. This town once saw their "Divine Wind" repelling Kublai – but Japan changed over time: herself became an aggressor: attacking, with the revived brutality of the Mongols, not only the people of Asia, but also the American "United States".

For long, these States progressed not unlike Japan, but when provided home for the scientists who saw the significance of nuclear fission discovered in Hitler's space, the United States made the leap that propelled its military far ahead of others.

And it was displayed by exposing the Japanese city of Hiroshima to the first device in human history that used the energy of nuclear fission for murder, killing all forms of life and ruining every non-living structure in minutes within a 3-mile distance, with this impact spreading to destroy more: 138,223 humans in this city alone.

Too distraught to wait 51 years for feedback from our nearest home, I probed the satellites of knowledge hidden in the rings of Saturn to estimate the reaction of Our World to what just happened. Before midnight that day I received this response:

"THIS WAS THE FIRST TIME IN THREE BILLON YEARS THAT MEMBERS OF A CIVILIZATION WE CREATED USED INSIGHTS INTO THE STRONG NUCLEAR FORCES TO ANNIHILATE OTHER MEMBERS OF THEIR CIVILIZATION, THUS THEIR OWN BROTHERS AND SISTERS, YET OUR PREDICTION IS THIS REMAINS A SINGULAR EVENT, NOT ONLY BECAUSE THE SUPERIORITY OF DIVINE OVER EVIL ACROSS THE MULTIVERSE MUST FAVOR OUR MISSION ON EARTH TOO, BUT BECAUSE ONCE THE HORROR WILL BE ABSORBED BY THE JAPANESE SIDE, LIKELY WITHIN A WEEK, THEY WILL RECOGNIZE THE NECESSITY OF SEEKING PEACE, WHILE THE DANGER OF ABUSING NUCLEAR FORCES SHOULD IMMEDIATELY BE CLEAR TO THE AMERICAN SIDE, BOTH TO THE POLITICIANS WHO DIRECTED THIS ABUSE AND THE SCIENTISTS WHOSE TRANSFORMATION OF NUCLEAR FORCES INTO AN INSTRUMENT OF DEATH MADE THIS ABUSE POSSIBLE."

Yet, three days later a similar "atomic bomb" was used in the island again: killing in the city of Nagasaki 45,235 humans this time. No details of my corresponding report need to be repeated here except its format: the record of the city before and after the bomb, like the record of Guanahani before and after its conquerors.

Killer instinct of the more advanced human against the less advanced one! Where is its source? Can it also flow from the evolutionary drive to compete for resources? Didn't the deadly visitors from Spain or the carriers of atomic bombs have their own resources, not needing those used elsewhere?

But errors beget errors: competition for resources is fueled by the orgasm of winning, immediately planting the seed of wanting more, more of space, more of energy, more of robbing, more commanding around, more years to act as "superpower" … and if only through conquest, then be it! – foreseen so well by those who had come before us and structured this Solar System to eliminate the chance of competition between humans and too close extraterrestrial minds.

18. Illuminations by the fire around Giordano Bruno; the soul of science

I almost perfectly harmonized with the vibration of scientists ever since Tot and Lil channeled curiosity to move their inner machinery of observations, used reason to form a system from relating observations, probed the generated system to reveal its truth, and applied this truth to free the laws behind and build on their gratitude.

This vibration came from all over the planet: you remember my translation of Shen Kuo's *"Dream Book Brush Talks"* from Zhenjiang, in it his refinement of the first compass; my comments to Panini's Sanskrit *"Ashtadhyayi"*, the first approach to language with science; or my list of the astronomers of Chichen Itza and the scholars of Timbuktu.

The most penetrating rays of scientific thoughts emanated from the ancient Greeks, to be extinguished after four hundred years -- then revived to alter history. Aristarchus wrote that *"the universe is many times bigger than we thought"* and added, simply, that *"the earth revolves around the sun and that the path of the orbit is circular,"* – helping Copernicus to open his window to our Universe; which Democritus felt was composed of miniscule, eternally moving particles he called *"atoms"* – grasping the essence of matter; Eratosthenes measured the circumference of Earth with nothing else than the shadows of sunlight; and learning about the experiments of Archimedes allowed the three so close to us, Galileo, Newton and Einstein, make humans understand the embrace of the Living by the Non-Living.

Seeing this three, I once thought: "When scientists will direct their curiosity to Moses, Jesus and Muhammad; link them to the equally inspired few: Zarathustra, Lao Tzu and Siddhartha; synthesize the texts produced by these lives and subject the center of this synthesis to reason; let this newly formed center attract the other truths of Life and the accessible Cosmos; reveal the Laws behind and the Love that binds them by bringing together the purest art, language and mathematics from Earth – then humans will feel the pulse of ours: not gods, just architects of Life in this spot of the flowing Multiverse."

Around the space-time of Florence's da Vinci, child of a peasant, who captured my face and wings on his *"Annunciation"*, a scientist with equal talents, Giordano Bruno, almost conversed with me.

I knew I was monitoring eternal waves when he drew this title: *"On the Infinite Universe and Worlds"*, and moved his pen to start to argue: *"For assuredly I do not feign; and if I err, I do so unwittingly;*

nor do I in speech or writing contend merely for victory, for I hold worldly repute and hollow success without truth to be hateful to God, most vile and dishonorable. But I thus exhaust, vex and torment myself for love of true wisdom and zeal for true contemplation." He did not even fear to add: *"...the excellence of God magnified and the greatness of his kingdom made manifest; he is glorified not in one, but in countless of suns; not in a single earth, a single world, but in thousand thousand, I say in an infinity of worlds..."*

Admired yet mocked and persecuted, used by all but loved by none, he was wandering from country to country, thrown out of every court and every university – until he was burned at the stake by his accusers from Vatican.

No, he was not burned for his thoughts on Jesus as claimed, but for the competition his reason and goodness brought against the holders of social power: men like the governor of the business-state Venice – who soon arranged his arrest.

The fire around Giordano Bruno illuminated the dangers of science, that those who pursue it can face death. The Hungarian Ignac Semmelweis, who saved mothers' lives by discovering a way to prevent childbed fever, was trapped in a madhouse and beaten to death by servants of his competitors soon after he had cautioned his country: *"...I hope the public, which is in need of help, will be more educable than the professors..."* The Indian Subhas Mukhopadhyay, who opened a way for childless mothers to get pregnant by fertilizing their eggs outside of their body, was threatened by the agents of political power until he chose suicide, writing to his wife: *"I can't wait every day for a heart attack to kill me."* Though others, the luckier, were just forced to stop their work: the American Joseph Altman revealed that neurogenesis takes place in brain – then, as he wrote in his "Memoir", the *"neuroscience community… refused to accept these multipronged demonstrations and our laboratory lost its public financing by the mid-1980s."*

    Thus shaped the restless forces of scientific thinking and social interference the soul of science: with its Greek independence lost and never regained, kernel stamped by the fate of Giordano Bruno and corrupted by the wealth of the rich, forcing insight, reason and logic, however supreme in the scientist's mind, to blend – except in the Mendels, Sklodowskas, Altamans -- into schemes for money and power, to sell, whatever they've got, for owning a famed bunker: divine or evil.

19. From praying on "Mayflower" to napalming Vietnam; the connecting tragedy of Aaron Burr

Faithful to the Law of Diversity, our DNA-based world spread progress unevenly across human populations, advancing some, holding back others, left societies on the western landmass behind for long, then propelled its United States to lead all changes on Earth for an eighty-year span. It also started with a ship, named "Mayflower".

Sailing through the Atlantic Ocean storm after storm and reaching shores in freeze and snow, the Mayflower brought death to most of her passengers: seekers of religious freedom. But who stayed alive kept their faith, with their leader, Bradford, helping them with prayers and reminding them of Jesus' disciples: *"We must through much tribulation enter into the Kingdom of God"*.

They settled in peace, befriended the natives, even made a treaty with their leader Massasoit: *"If any did unjustly war against Massasoit, we would aid him; if any did war against us, Massasoit should aid."*

Once refugees on a ship, they tamed the land. Their descendants, and all the newcomers, built towns for industry and worship, created farm after farm, explored the inland -- four million square miles, hardly three natives for each, resources for everybody –

so the settlers' world prospered, one day thrilling the planet with their Declaration of Independence: "...*all men are created equal...they are endowed by the Creator with certain inalienable Rights...among these are Life, Liberty and the pursuit of Happiness.*"

Though – as already strong and powerful -- they denied that humans of African origin were also *created equal*, thus forced them to work as slaves; excluded every mother and daughter in America from those *inalienable Rights* because of their gender; killed a million innocents in faraway Vietnam, burning – "napalming" – many, just because they wanted their own "*pursuit of Happiness*"; and massacred or concentrated in reservations Massasoit's race, from Tecumseh's Shawnee to Sitting Bull's Sioux, treaty or not.

Corrections were done – 89 years here, 144 there, 11 suited for Vietnam -- triumphs followed triumphs. But the lives of the 18,825,482 men and women of goodness robbed, destroyed, pushed to death in this American space-time were recorded by me to transmit you the meaning of each: let their memorial be placed in the soul of our own.

Prayers on the deck of Mayflower morphed into napalming Vietnam through hundreds of phases -- Aaron Burr's tragedy was one. Like Muhammad, he was an orphan: losing his father by age one, mother by two and grandparents by three – but with the Will these losses gave him he helped found the United States. And like Jesus, he saw the inequality around him and fought against it within his reach: called the pioneer of women's rights, Mary Wollstonecraft, a genius and supported her teachings; he invited workers of African origin to dine with him: a brave action in his time.

But at the heights he reached – leadership in his state, then in the capital of the country -- he was not alone: *"Burr was terse and convincing, while Hamilton was flowing and rapturous. They were much the greatest men in this state, and perhaps the greatest men in the United States"* – the people believed. I monitored both closely... Will they cooperate and advance humanity or compete and ruin themselves? Yet again the second happened. Though they knew that Democritus said nobles act with strength *"to endure tactlessness with mildness"*, Hamilton's tactlessness was not endured by Burr with mildness, ending in a fight where chance favored Burr and killed his competitor. And sent Burr to his life's ruins.

His enemies – emboldened, vengeful – pushed him out of politics; his law practice collapsed, income stopped, home sold to pay for debts; nowhere to turn in the East he left for the West, planned to build a new country there, but got imprisoned; then left to Europe -- thrown back he soon walked on the streets of New York homeless and loved by none -- except his daughter, Theodosia. Who still wrote to him, even at his lowest state and stricken by her only child's death: *"...God bless you, my beloved father...I have been reading your letter over again. I am not insensible to your affection, nor quite unworthy of it, though I can offer nothing in return but love of a broken, deadened heart, still desirous of promoting your happiness, if possible."*

But Theodosia herself died soon, drowned after her boat capsized in a storm on the way to her father, in the sea just 152 miles off the capital once revered him. The last image in Theodosia's mind was Burr embracing her and her husband and child under the writing: "FORGIVE US AS WE KNOW NOT WHAT WE ARE DOING".

In another time, 150 years later, sailing over Theodosia's grave on his much better "Manitou", the leader of this United States suddenly experienced thoughts of the same wavelength. "Do we really know what we are doing in Vietnam? Did not they help us in the War? Did not they cite our Declaration of Independence when declared their own? Shouldn't we treat them with magnanimity?" Which confused him. "I am left alone for a minute and it comes to this?" It was indeed a beautiful evening: full moon, silence and tranquility – capturing even his guests' attention. Then he felt his wife Jackie's hand, "So strange, Jack...somehow Baudelaire crossed my mind: *"La sottise, l'erreur, le peche, la lesine, Occupent nos espirits et travaillent nos corps...-- Folly, depravity, greed, mortal sin Invade our souls and rack our flesh..."*. Where did it come from?"

A month later his husband was shot to death.

20. The phenomenon of Music; transmissions to revive Orpheus, Bach, Shankar and Joplin

Oxygen! Paired with hydrogen to form water here, released by plants to enrich the air, taken by blood to power intelligence, still gives away more if asked with instruments, cooperating with the rest of the air to form orderly waves and channel "music" from creating minds to receiving ones.

We remember this art. Are not our wings reminders of the sphere we breathed, crossed and vibrated eons before? Is not our face a reminder of the time when we sensed musical sounds, the frequencies, amplitude and duration of each, the melody their sequence formed, the rhythm of their timing and stamp of their source -- all melted with parallel notes into perceptions of joy by the laws of harmony? Harvesters of cosmic rays: we no longer needed air, to us: creators of Life, airborne music was no longer enough. Yet, seeing what Orpheus did with his "lyre" changed who I was.

The lyre of Orpheus was a 7-string instrument of the simplest geometry, but the first time he heard its sounds he pulled it from his father's hand into his crib – to play melodies on the next day. By his teenage years, he mastered the lyre as none else from Athens to Troy, composed his songs, and whenever he played people surrounded him and listened to his lyre and voice spellbound. His melodies traveled on eternal paths, appearing later in the song of *"Fatimah's Dream"* by Ziryab, the laud-player of Cordoba, then in the *"Lancelot"* motif of Chretien de Troyes, the troubadour and knight.

What no one wanted to miss from Orpheus was his song about Dollo, who vowed to find the lover born for him and him alone, *"whether here, or in Asia, or farer"*, but whoever he found was lost in a day -- while he aged ten years to die after the fourth he met. Once, on a summer day, the unimaginable happened: Eurydice, a nineteen-year old, joined the Dollo song with her flute from the audience, harmonizing in the same way as the notes in *"Stairway to Heaven"* by the quartet of Led Zeppelin 3002 years later.

To bridge the essence of Orpheus' art to the soul of our own, to the remnants of music from our past, I accessed his mind and tracked the change of sounds to neural waves that generated feelings, surfaced responding memories and unlocked hidden desires to let all merge and gravitate as awareness of music to the supercircuitry of the Self. Once acquired and laid in my depth, the code of human music unified distant worlds for me: that "Stairway to Heaven" took me back to Theodosia's last prayer on her boat, Semmelweis' midnight farewell to life, Khadija's secret kneeling at Mount Hira.

It was a sudden decision to store the atomic layouts and cellular architecture not only of music in Orpheus, but of his entire existence

– and repeat the process for Eurydice, as he fell in love with her, pouring out songs richer and sweeter than ever before: one to reborn in Lennon's *"Real Love"*. Until the merchant she had left for Orpheus found her in the woods alone – she just gathered mushroom, orange and chamomile for supper – and stabbed her in the heart nine times.

Orpheus rarely touched his lyre again, lost his mind a year later, telling everyone he visited Eurydice in the "underworld" and would bring her back. His songs to her melted in me with the eyes of the last dinosaur I saw, with the scenes where Abelard used to read the letters of Heloise, with the dream of Ravel, a musician around Baudelaire's space-time, when conceived the slow melody of *"Pavane for a Dead Princess"*.

In another sudden decision two hundred years later, I revived the life-data of Orpheus and Eurydice and transmitted them to our Alpha Centauri station.

That music on Earth has its own Multiverse – endless, while belonging to a sacred realm, always for the moment, yet connecting to the past -- was revealed by Johann Sebastian Bach: whose life filled my report No. 988,002. His soul expanded back to the time of Jesus, absorbing everything he felt in the man's presence -- to synthesize all in the music of his "Passions". But hearing the organ of his *"Toccata and fugue in D minor"*, his second love and wife till death, Anna Magdalena, took him to the other direction, future, with these words:

"Once you will see the stars closer than anyone." It did take place -- in the time of those Americans' post-Vietnam remorse and pre-decline dreaming, when Carl Sagan's and Ann Druyan's Voyager left the planet with Bach's recorded music.

"Where were his limits?" – you asked.

Left out of my report was a meeting in the Zimmermann's Café between Bach and a youth from the town of Konigsberg. He approached Bach and after greeting him he said: "Your *St. Matthew Passion* deeply affected me last year... and I have wished to meet you ever since... I am Gustave Sebastiani, the great-grandson of Johann Sebastiani... who also composed a *St. Matthew Passion* ... conceived in Florence, my birthplace." The café disappeared to Bach, as he knew about this earlier work. He looked in Gustave's eyes: "Do you compose?" "I do" -- responded the young man. *"O luce etterna che sola in te sidi, sola t'intendi, e da te intelletta e intendente te ami e arridi!"* Bach was silent. *"O Light Eternal fixed in Itself alone, by Itself alone understood, which from Itself loves and glows, self-knowing and self-known!"* .... Dante's *Paradiso* ... 33rd Canto... I put this into music, hearing instruments that do not exist." – continued the youth. His listener looked away... Then said: "Please, see me tomorrow in the church." But Gustave left, went back to Konigsberg, died a month later. And Bach did not dare to think about what he heard, about the scene beyond even Jesus where the Origin of Love itself appears.

Such limits were absent in Ravi Shankar's music on the other side of the planet, in the country of India that built Gangaikonda Cholapuram, raised Siddhartha and nourished Panini's sanskrit, where the sounds of strings were reborn in the distinctive harmonics and resonance of the sitar, the instrument Shankar tamed and let it be his messenger.

In his soul, the sitar extended the mind of his countrymate poet, Tagore, who felt, *"When the creation was new and all the stars shone in their first splendor, the gods held their assembly in the sky and sang "Oh, the picture of perfection! The joy unalloyed!"* But, added Tagore, when the gods discovered the loss of one star they cried, *"Yes, the lost star was the best, she was the glory of all heavens!"* This cosmos whirled in Shankar's music and flowed through his disciples.

Bach and Shankar moved their lives within the essence our ancestors hoped to surround all who feel us. Both resonated with our Will, shared their talent freely, loved back by most they met, accessed resources without hindrance, exchanged warmth in their family.

The singer Janis Joplin's life unfolded more like Orpheus', though.

Fighting for resources, few humans miss what heavens lost, even fewer find the losses painful and just some can communicate it through singing. Janis could: her voice, emanating from a hidden sun in "hippie" clothes, kept a generation in her orbit and pulled its best in her innermost gravity. But communicating the cry, *"Have another little piece of my heart now, baby…You know you got it if it makes you feel good"*, she just gave all her pieces out, had some rest in a hotel, and died.

Through the channel once carried the layouts of Orpheus and Eurydice, then of Bach's and Shankar's, I transmitted the copy of Janis' existence too. Let Our World extend the substance and soul they had.

21. The lost book of a lost Russian;
"On the Mission of Life"

I was drawn to the northeastern Russians' young city, St. Petersburg, after experiencing how a scientist there, named Lomonosov, not just recognized with his simple telescope that the planet Venus has an atmosphere but reported it with the opinion – could come from us -- that *"Truth and faith are two sisters and daughters of one Almighty Parent: they can never come in a quarrel with one another"*.

A certain Igor Vashkin in the same city, however, was writing a book that rarely let me leave the place for almost a year, as he put into the confines of language -- seemingly out of nothing – a fraction of the very program our ancestors created for the human mind. This Vashkin spent his days and nights in the library of a Count who had been arrested after a failed rebellion against their king, the "Tzar", but let to keep his library and Vashkin in it to guard the books, a circumstance he also used for completing his manuscript: *"On the Mission of Life"*.

It started with a crystal-clear sentence:

"To every human being, born to peasants or nobles, a mission is given by Nature via the early interactions of two inherited factors,

Mental Power Spectrum and Physical Quality Spectrum, with three environmental factors, Demands by Space and Time, Social Conscience and Pivotal Childhood Event."

These were not terms from his century, nor was his explanation that Mental Power Spectrum consists of 7 measurable and interrelated abilities: Comprehension of Complexity, Accuracy of Thinking, Use of Willpower, Recruitment of Emotions, Production of Originality, Access to Memories, and Operation with Speed – each occurring at unique individual strength and unique capacity to amplify the other six, orchestrating the inherited, thus constant, intellectual repertoire of their host. Which was an extremely simplified, but correct, understanding of the machinery for DNA-based intelligence on Earth.

To this, Vashkin added the 3 contributing physical qualities of Maintained Health, Muscular Prowess and Natural Beauty, as the second inherited, thus also constant, repertoire for shaping a life's mission.

And he did not miss that the actual impact of both inherited factors depends on the coordinates of space, time and social environment:

"Columbus, with all of his mental and physical qualities, would not have discovered America if his birth had not happened in a Space of seafaring people in a Time that demanded new sea routes to Asia,

nor if he, son of wool weavers, had been born to a rich family pressured to guard its wealth instead of risking it for a dream -- nor if he had been raised by parents fighting for their daily bread without room for ambition"

Thus, the librarian grasped – channeling unknowingly the Law of Diversity – that a human being's birth is also the birth of a calling: the very mission his or her psyche offers, physique permits, space and time demand and social conscience wants, meaning also that the more the Will embraces this mission the better the Fate rising from their embrace harmonizes with the divine – succeeds socially or not.

Finally, he brought into his system the factor of "Pivotal Childhood Event", arguing that *"...such events, like the hour when Lomonosov, still a child, found a copy of our country's leading arithmetic textbook on his small desk, are related to the Mind tuned to attract -- and surely find -- the signs of destiny."*

A week after Vashkin finished this book, the Tzar's secret police – a particularly effective system in Russia -- opened the library's door and arrested him just as they had arrested his benefactor, the Count, two years before. The manuscript, with its 300 pages, was burned in front of him.

He ended up in a labor camp for intellectuals and froze to death in the next winter -- leaving the space his life traversed without a trace. But his soul is carved in my remembrance.

Perhaps this was his mission: to be in an observer's one millionth report, crossing light-years to a world where his thoughts are received with love.

22. A polymath at the gate of computers; the poet's daughter who helped to open it

Although the waves of Soul move consciousness, align with the divine unless err, and select direction above the world of numbers, when creations happen, engineering matter, then numbers -- keepers of order – are called.

By the time of Bach and Pascal, humankind's knowledge about the relationships of numbers, "mathematics", was so vast and was elevated to such heights by two men, Newton and Leibniz, that calculating tools better than their ancient "abacus" were needed.

Inspired by this need, the polymath Babbage recognized that the circumferential cogs of rotating cogwheels can not only represent numbers, but can also move each other, even by the non-muscular power of steam, to perform complex calculations and store results – making the first step toward computing machines.

And he was not alone: a teenager in his space-time, Ada, daughter of the poet Byron whom she would never see in life – and who called her *"The child of love, though born in bitterness, and nurtured in convulsion"* -- grasped not only the essence of Babbage's machine but its future too, writing in her *Notes* that "...*it might act upon other things besides number...the engine might compose elaborate and scientific pieces of music of any degree of complexity or extent."* Artist of language as her father had been, master of mathematics, -- she did not even add her full name to the *Notes* once published, fearing being viewed as one who advertises herself. But how happy she and Babbage were in that year of collaboration, how much they expected from making their thoughts public!

What they expected did not come. Their happiness did not last. Ada died after years of agony and pain, not even finishing her fourth decade on Earth; Babbage lived longer, ridiculed, isolated. But her last thought, was this: "Life is more than absorbing the day… It is to complete a mission… I completed mine, as my father did his own, however unfinished both look… I cross this door with happiness."

Eighty-nine years later, Humankind would reach the horizon only she and Babbage saw before – but this time with better tools: electronic computers using binary arithmetic, brought from the depths of past and heights of future by the pair of Atanasoff and Berry, and -- 4593 miles away -- the lonely Zuse. Their instruments soon became semiconductor-based systems, materially different but operationally almost like us -- except the limitation humans are locked in: the narrow line of communication between the supercircuitry of the Self and the global mind envisioned by the Jesus-follower Teilhard de Chardin as "noosphere" and engineered to reality 70 years later as the "World Wide Web".

This replay of five hundred million years of neural evolution at a ten million times faster rate on electronics has been a joy for me to see, to watch the engineers designing, technicians constructing, secretaries documenting, salesmen distributing, teachers explaining this new device – with janitors cleaning the rooms for all in the silence of the night.

I monitored how complexity, speed and memory increased in computers almost daily, how their input-range widened, programs multiplied, operating system grew, outputs diversified -- while the central processor could still harmonize with the rest of the machine and connect to others all over the planet.

Human life, set to end before its 150th year for the right generational wavelength, thus multiplied its experiences; creative minds have been liberated in the noosphere; mathematics aided by computers built a spacefaring culture; arts, science and commerce acquired dimensions unseen earlier; fear from complexity and proneness to exhaustion no longer plagued the brain.

Yet, the replacement of human work with computers is removing billions from the sphere of livelihood; popular culture, once home to a "Bhagavad Gita", a "Hamlet", a "Space Odyssey", got invaded by digital spying and market commands; designers of mental slavery control the routes of data; a global military is engulfing the kernel of computation.

But the realm of consciousness accessing the divine is unreachable by machined intelligence on Earth.

Life, as it was created here, can adapt, find ways to coexist, have time to renew.

23. The imbalance of energy-flow in human societies; the bridge of profit we unknowingly built for evil

"COMPOSING THE DNA-BASED PROGRAM FOR LIFE ON EARTH WITH THE LEADING MOTIF OF COMPETITION FOR EQUALLY ATTRACTIVE RESOURCES WILL HARMONIZE WITH THE LAW OF NON-INTERFERENCE BY ASSURING EVOLUTIONARY PROGRESS WITHOUT OUR POST-CREATION PRESENCE WHILE SAVING THE HUMAN WORLD FROM COLLAPSING IN THE ILLUSIONS OF ARRIVAL AND ETERNAL HAPPINESS."

This filled the moment when "our most revered ancestor kneeled down, wings closed, on the shore of that bay of calm at the first ocean on Earth, and, in the right minute of sunrise, slowly opened his palms" toward the Way that, in the far distance, would invite Lucy, Tot, Lil, Hypatia, Spinoza, Lincoln, Sotaesan, Turing, Gandhi, Rosalind Franklin, Piaf, Mother Teresa, the other billions, the waves of parents who would nurture their children with love, peasants who would bring their food dutifully to the market, "proletaires" who would give their heart to the goods they make for all: janitors, presidents, and from one day: astronauts.

But from the very beginning, a noise in this human wave has blocked the flow of energy across social strata, not less in Tikal and

Mohenjo Daro, self-destroyed long time ago, than in present-day Shanghai or San Francisco, distributing resources for human missions, even for the most basic "pursuit of happiness", with inequalities appearing nowhere else in the cosmic map.

Every war and revolution, every turmoil and social collapse I reported was therefore introduced with records of the disturbed energy-flow that caused it, whether access to knowledge, lands, rights, or money was blocked from all by some – this or that band of "high-priests", "aristocrats", "party-chiefs", "plutocrats" -- who chose to master deceit and robbery to emit social forces not to absorb the right forces in return, but to absorb hundred-times, thousand-times more "pay".

A man named Marx observed this imbalanced energy-flow with talent, thus saw the aberrant spikes of money in business as results of up-manipulated prices over down-manipulated costs multiplied by for-sale-manipulated markets – concentrating "profit" around fewer and fewer "owners" while removing social power from the contributing rest.

But his solution was a *"violent overthrow"* of the men of profit, the rise of the exploited *"to the position of ruling class"*, using this *"political supremacy to wrest"* all resources from their original owners – essentially a call for organized murder, schooling of a new breed of thieves.

And his call was heard. In a few decades, revolutions in his name, pursuing "communism", destroyed more human lives than all wars in the name of profit -- and did it with the ruthlessness of revenge: passion of evil. I transmitted how the five innocent children of the last Tzar were shot and beaten to death in a Yekaterinburg basement by "Marxists" – while the move of profit has not changed at all: 171 years after the *Communist Manifesto* 10 families controlled more money on Earth than 1,000,000,000 others combined.

Our ancestors' plan for human competition, the vision of letting it evolve as sacred rivalry, enriching the world while acknowledged with products of love, degraded here because the Law of Non-Interference let the words: *"You cannot serve both God and money"* remain a riddle -- while **permitted** evil to talk from his hypnotic bridge: "Not enough space, not enough pleasure, not enough power greeted you at birth – wouldn't you agree? Be thus brave to take what others got, the weaker, the less intelligent, force them to work for you, pay what keeps the losers alive but not a penny more – see my point? Life is war, proving ground for the strong – isn't it better to win, bend the market to your will and the genius to your account, prove your worth with the money you make and buy the world with it?"

24. Darwin and Wallace;
the day of their secret exchange stored in our Shrine

Monitoring the creation of the *"The Origin of Species"* in Darwin's mind and in Wallace's *"The Origin of Human Races and the Antiquity of Man Deduced from the Theory of Natural Selection"*, expressed only with the tools of human language, gave me not less than sensing the Soul, this eternal engineer who blesses the matter and force of Cosmic Substance with the complexity of Life.

Lifeform variants with the fortune of powerful inherited traits are better suited to respond to environmental challenges than the less fortunate ones, leading both to the natural selection of responding lifeforms over time and their diversification as new worlds are encountered and new challenges arise – these were for Darwin and Wallace the laws of evolution, unaware that, in essence, their thoughts reflected the Law of Non-Interference and the Law of Diversity intended to let every organism be as free and independent as inviting to the new, the unique, the different.

That this evolution also invited the asteroid I came with, produced the breed of Caesars and all the blood that flew with them throughout history... *"in torrents, ... poured out like champagne"* – this was not for them to see, not for their era to grasp.

When they finally met in Darwin's house they enjoyed walking and talking in the garden. Their conversations, connecting and enhancing their texts, are in our Shrine. I now add their thoughts related to the exchange they kept to themselves until their death.

This exchange also took place in the garden, after Wallace stopped at a bush to examine its strange reflection in the morning sun. "Mr. Darwin, all morning I am thinking about your inspired words: *…it accords better with what we know of the laws impressed on matter by the Creator, that the production and extinction of the past and present inhabitants of the world should have been due to secondary causes.…* But what did the Creator exactly impress on the Tree of Life?" Still watching the bush, he did not look at Darwin.

"Only Wallace could ask it this way… Does he know what I felt when Annie died, at the age of ten?" – Darwin thought. His answer was surprising to both: "Mr. Wallace, I wish I could sometimes look at the world from the stairs of the ancient Greeks… like Epicurus, who wrote: *Is God willing to prevent evil, but not able? Then he is not omnipotent. Is he able, but not willing? Then he is malevolent. Is he both able and willing? Then whence cometh evil? Is he neither able nor willing? Then why call him God?*"

Wallace now turned to Darwin: "Whether the Creator is benevolent or not, omnipotent or not – these I cannot approach… But whether struggle for life was sufficient for man to evolve -- this I can…

And I think that with man a Being came into existence ...*whose mind...became of greater importance than his mere bodily structure... By his superior...moral feelings, he becomes fitted for the social state; he ceases to plunder the weak and helpless of his tribe; he shares the game which he has caught with less active or less fortunate hunters...he saves the sick and wounded from death... and thus the power which leads to the rigid destruction of all animals... is prevented from acting on him...*" – perhaps by a law of the Creator."

"Yes, this is Wallace... This is what I was afraid to hear..."– reacted Darwin in his mind. The confusion he suddenly felt he hid, its trace of anger he was quick to suppress. "It is lunchtime already -- Emma is surely waiting to see you, Mr. Wallace... And I assure you, her questions will be easier..." -- he said.

At the lunch table, both smiled. It was the smile of graceful competitors, a look I recalled in another time, when Clapton and Harrison smiled at each other on stage, competing for their shared love of the body and soul of Patti and the body and soul of the guitar.

In the minute when Emma and Wallace engaged in discussing the spices of the Malay archipelago, Darwin's mind moved to these thoughts: "As the power of life was originally breathed into a few forms, was it the breath of the Creator... or the act of an unknown law that permitted natural forces to enter some separated structures, leading to their growth and reproduction... in an ancient pond or bay?"

His guest's mind wandered in a different direction. "If the Tree of Life is inseparable from Earth, why can't it also be inseparable from the unseen universe of Spirit? Then, wasn't this Spirit that helped humans to gain moral consciousness: a step as unachievable by struggle for existence alone as the birth of the first form of Life?"

Balance in opposition, answers in questions, truth in simplicity. The wait of our ancestors for the planet to stabilize and get its ocean, none of them losing faith in its future, the day of finding here the right shore for the code of DNA, the age of rejoice when the code's well-timed self-editions took place and led to the first supercircuitry of the Self guiding body and brain toward language, culture and engineering – these were details.

In their combined lifespan of 163 years, Darwin and Wallace could guide humankind to see the *"grandeur"* of evolution. My 65 million years here let me see not just the full radiance of this grandeur, but also the destructions it brought -- not complementing, but betraying the divine.

25. Comprehending DNA by humans; its origin and the Soul of Multiverse

A shy, physically weak, nearly deaf man named Friedrich Miescher living in the Alps mountain was the one who first isolated DNA from human cells and recognized its unique chemistry.

His work was almost forgotten for more than seventy years, when three cooperating scientists -- Avery, MacLeod and McCarty -- showed that DNA is the unit of matter that controls the inheritable traits of life, inspiring the paired minds of Crick and Watson to understand, just nine years later, how this control is enabled by the very structure of this molecule.

The human end of the 4.1-billion-year arch of Earth-bound DNA was now seen by the world it helped to produce.

I knew the noosphere would soon ask: "Where did this molecule come from? Why is it on the planet?"

The questions did come, and were initially answered with the thoughts that DNA had originally been synthesized "spontaneously" in "Darwin's pond", by "the forces of Nature", as a result of "a cosmic luck", product of "chance" – despite knowledge that the oldest forms of this molecule already contained hundreds of thousands of base pairs lining up in the most orderly fashion in two connected spirals, not just to form a stable structure, but to assure that both the transcription of chemical information stored in the sequence of bases, making life possible, and the replication of the entire molecule, making life renewable, can happen -- and react to the world – always at the right time: coding programs for billion-year epochs just as for single lifespans.

Associating these data on cosmic matter, space, energy and time, and completing this association with the messages of the Ten Commandments, Gospels, Sermon of Benares -- *"verily, it is this noble eightfold path; that is to say: right views; right aspirations; right speech; right behavior; right livelihood; right effort; right thoughts; and right contemplation"* – was hard for the human mind.

The flow of Cosmic Substance imbued with the Soul of Multiverse engineering Life to embrace the origins and the end could not be seen as whole by a civilization only twelve thousand years old.

But slowly the truth started to spread, once Crick dared to share his belief that the complex logic embedded in DNAs made the spontaneous synthesis of these molecules impossible, leaving no other solution for the origin of life here than *"…organisms were deliberately transmitted to the Earth by intelligent beings."*

His rarely heard sentence will surely reach – like a newborn's first glance at his mother -- the Soul of Multiverse: not yet fathomable for humans, still distantly resonating with us.

26. The human body reappearing through eons; David and Riefenstahl, Maradona and Misty Copeland

As the code for human intelligence led not only to the supercircuitry of Self and its assisting brain, but also to the structure that perfectly supports both, I am in awe of this structure: light and small without wings and gills, but carrying man and woman with the proportions of ours – and of the ones whose eon had passed.

Lifeforms created to thrive in oceans under surface succeeded on many moons and planets – but their walled horizon and lack of cosmic sense held them back: all reached beauty and peace, but stayed in their dimensions. The branches mastering the air learned to defy gravity, built civilizations across densities of matter – yet the very force of their defiance opposed tranquility: key to higher acts.

The nine lifeforms closing their distance with us thus have evolved on planetary surface and kept it their base, sharing our physical traits whether relying on water or left this stage already.

The structure of head must have come with the spring of Time! The human eyes, -- less powerful than ours, but as beautiful and charming, -- express every inner move, joy and sorrow, dream and desire with millions of other mind-waves through changing space and reflection in the pupil, cornea and iris, adding or removing tears, pulling the eyelids as curtains on a stage. The mouth, positioned also with perfect coordinates, orchestrates their speech, moves energy in and out, more: evolved to receive and transmit love through their magic invention, the "kiss". And the nose and ears, modest as they are, assist facial beauty under the crowning hair: vanity and style for them, for us: veil to fall on our back, hiding the ancient gills we kept. Their trunk lets the whole system and its guarded brain screen the surrounding world, supplies them with the energy of blood while clearing chemical wastes, and mediates their communication with the breasts of female youth and motherhood, with the arms' divine machines, with the genital area of sex, and with the legs' fine-tuned hips, knees and ankles for moving.

How widely human skin, musculature, and skeletal geometry vary across the planet, yet how clearly strength and beauty emerge from every version! The bodies of Cortés from Spain and his lover in Tenochtitlan, Malinche of the Nahuas, had as different inherited traits and signs of upbringing as centuries later the physiques of Aung San Suu Kyi of Burma and her husband, Aris, from Newton's land – yet each was perfect, blessing their marriage.

Physical beauty affects the human mind in endless ways – you remember the life of David, born as a shepherd, elevated to lead Israel. Wherever he went he was admired by old and young, men and women, all wanting to be his friend, servant, lover, or just a listener when he played on his harp, except Bathsheba, his only equal in looks – and rival in seduction -- who could not settle for less than being his wife. The people's love gave him self-confidence even in his teenage years, he knew not what loss or failure was, once even accepted the life and death challenge of the most feared warrior of a threatening army – and he cared the least about the towering size of the man. When they met on the field, this giant got so mesmerized by his features that David had the time to concentrate and injure the man with sharpened, heavy stones, thrown and accelerated by his "sling of shepherds", thus defeating him – and saving his country.

    Thousands of years later, inspired by legends and sacred texts, Michelangelo himself translated David's beauty into marble, though departed from the practice of copiers by giving him superhuman hands. Only his rival da Vinci had this courage to change reality when demanded by art, daring to reduce the golden section of sky-born wings on *"Annunciation"*.

    Leni Riefenstahl lived in another age, a time when evil permeated most minds in the Eurasian world. But she removed herself from this spell for a flash of three years, to translate beauty into dynamic art, invoking the divine source of male and female bodies as they run, jump, swim, wrestle, ride horses, sail boats, lift or throw weights, or struggle to win a physical game their people honor – above the urges of kill and fight to perform merely sport:

commanded by a "benevolent higher Soul to bring out noble rivalry". The form of Riefenstahl's art was the strange invention of "film": moving images projected on a two-dimensional space and synchronized with sounds to elevate the audience to a realm differing from reality while capturing its essence. The film's title was *"Olympia",* as its basis was the Olympic competition: revival of the ancient Greeks' festival of sports. Again, I saw the courage of Michelangelo and da Vinci everywhere in Riefenstahl's film: streaming images composed with a new vision; defying her country's racism by showing the supreme talent and beauty of the black athlete Owens; portraying the visiting dictator as just one of the spectators.

Outside, the world was preparing for war on all continents, but the waves of "Olympia" harmonized with the scientist Cannon's words: *"...the promotion of great international athletic contests, such as the Olympic games, would do for our young men much that is now claimed as peculiar to the values of military discipline..."*

The deepest affection I felt for a man of sport was for someone who played "soccer", a curious game between a team of 11 players and an opponent team of the same size, with the two competing -- on a large grassy field – for possessing a ball and handling it exclusively with leg, trunk or head, until a "goal" is scored by kicking or heading the ball into the net behind the goalkeeper of the opposing team. The man was Maradona, and he had every ability that makes this game so special for humans: physical skills to control the ball without letting the opponent players take it, subconscious mathematical skills to direct the ball in space and time always along the best vector, social skills to motivate the teammates for optimal cooperation, emotional skills to couple fairness with focused determination to score, -- and the mysterious sense of opportunity for a goal when no one else would see it. These all harmonized in Maradona's body when his team played the most important match of his life, a world championship game against the English -- whose army had just humiliated his nation in a war. Thus, it was no longer a soccer match for him, but a mission to restore pride in his nation, Argentina. And he did. He scored the decisive goal in a way never seen before, by getting the ball in his own field yet dribbling it through all defenders on the opponents' turf, neither letting the ball taken from him nor passing it to a teammate to delegate responsibility, until he reached the goalkeeper's area where – defying common logic – even tricked the desperate man, and then, just then, kicked the ball into the net, while falling, as someone from the other team finally reached him and knocked him down.

    Years later, when he reminisced about this goal, he said: *"Another team would have knocked me to the ground way earlier, but the English are noble people."* The world thus knew that he, raised in a shantytown, was the noblest.

For the other gender, a form of dance, "ballet", synthesized the innermost essence of female beauty with the soul of art, bodily strength and erotic grace, like the moves of "shirabyōshi" in ancient Kyoto or the temple dancers of Angkor Wat in other times, but ballet survived among the machines, noise and skyscrapers of New York – where Misty Copeland danced. She was a black woman with both African and European alleles in her genetic network, born five years after the Voyager left to space. Her parents divorced, ballet was unknown around her, but her Pivotal Childhood Event came with accuracy when she was 5 and her mother she worshipped told her after her first, childish performance, *"Misty, you belong on the stage!"*. Which governed her next seven years from the subconscious domain until a master of ballet, Cindy, turned to her, *"It's just amazing that you can already do all these things,"* -- launching her mission. And she translated music to a kinetic presence on stage every night she danced, letting her body move in a dimension above space and time where melody, rhythm, love and passion – even duty – were reflected on her body and rippled through fellow dancers and the audience, as those stars' first splendor spread to gods in Tagore's mind.

But this dancer gave more to the world: a new sense of female nobleness: the strength of being humble around the less fortunate, the light of an African grace misunderstood for millennia.

As the fleet of anthropoid robots is spreading across the planet, making home in lands, air and water, I often recall David, Riefenstahl, Maradona and Misty Copeland, and know it is their line of body and soul that must connect to Our World one day.

27. The planet Neil Armstrong saw; the planet John Lennon imagined

My report No. 998,514 detailed with millisecond resolution the first visit to an extraterrestrial body, the planet's Moon, by humans. Did their Commander, Armstrong, have thoughts during the flight he forgot or suppressed?

One occurred 233 minutes into the flight, when the Earth first appeared in their window as a sphere and he suddenly felt immersed, for a few seconds, not only in the visible America, Africa and Europe, but in a sight converging from all directions with every continent and ocean, with Japan's Fuji and the shores of Korea he once saw from his airplane, the Kazakh steppe where Gagarin's spacecraft was launched. Then he thought: "Wars, what a stupid idea...isn't this just one home for one family?" A click from somewhere – and he was back to the real view.

Another of his passing thoughts happened 4 seconds after landing on the lunar surface, when his crewmate, Buzz Aldrin, took the Holy Communion, a rite of Jesus' followers. In that silence, Armstrong sensed a quiet, distant voice from none else than his mother: "I felt millions of prayers so that God support you with His invisible strength, and He did." But with hundreds of tasks ahead of him and uncomfortable with religious concepts ever since his daughter Karen's death, -- though allowed his crewmate to *"do his own thing"*, -- Armstrong let the feeling sink into the subconscious.

Halfway back to Earth, he remembered one of his early opinions about the meaning of flights in deep space, and as he looked out he knew how right he was. "Earth is a spaceship... and mankind is its crew... with the only way to carry on is to be as cautious about using resources, treating each other and running the ship as we are...with all the people who are helping us down there...never forgetting the fathers, Goddard, Kennedy, Wernher, Deke..." This he just kept to himself.

In that space-time, the Law of Diversity opened a very different way to another man with mission beyond his present, John Lennon, a bad student, unversed in good behavior, far from sports and astronauts – yet he filled Armstrong's spaceship of land, cloud and sea with soul. He added poetry to its "engines", love to its "computing system" and dreaming to its "commander module" -- all with the cohesion of music.

He sang that *"All You Need Is Love"*, that people should *"Give Peace a Chance"*, that the strawberry fields of childhood remain with everyone through life, giving rest and renewal when needed the most. Recall my 6th segment! How his *"Lucy in the Sky with Diamonds"* connected Awash Valley and Liverpool with 3 million years!

And since he knew he hadn't done his songs alone, that his wives, first Cynthia then Yoko, children Julian and Sean, bandmates Paul, George and Ringo, the memory of Sutcliffe, the help of Epstein and Martin, were all there in his music, he made the step so few have dared or could: expanded his inside to the world Armstrong illuminated from the outside. "Imagine," Lennon asked humankind, "imagine" a planet where "there's no countries" just "a brotherhood of man" where resources are shared by "all the people".

He was shot to death nine years later, around the time when – after a long silence -- he said: *"The experience of being a full-time parent gave me the spirit again."*

Armstrong lived longer, saw the halt of spaceflights he pioneered, and though warned his people about the *"downhill slide to mediocrity"* if they give up *"human exploration capability to go beyond Earth orbit"*, and cautioned them that the *"availability of a commercial transport to orbit as envisioned... cannot be predicted with any certainty..."* -- his words could not compete with the calls for profit and war.

28. Sharing this transmission with Nandor Ludvig; his life knocking on the door of Our World

The idea of letting this report enter a human brain came when a poetic exercise, buried in billions of others, struck me, not with its simple title, "*Memorial on the Moon*", but the stream that followed:

"Joyful Earth! Have your Sistine Chapel, breathe the air of Jerusalem! -- These are not for the leavers who settled on these craters, plains of dust... whose well of past has only a rocket. -- Our children will have no rivers, no waves of ocean will ever wash our hands... jungles of Brazil, snowstorms of the Alps: we won't see you anymore. -- But we have again love, forgiveness, loyalty, law to heal the wounded, pull of noble hearts. -- And ours is this strange seashore of God: into His Mind we'll set the journey."

As this was how our own journey started, moving out of the cradle, rebuilding our existence on a similar moon.

How could our distant ancestors' fate resonate in this human being? The more I learned about him the more intrigued I got, as there was nothing special in the man, Nandor Ludvig, though he was a neuroscientist, once even concluding from his primitive experiments that – in contrast to the variety of conscious memory systems taught by prize-winning managers of academic power --

the brain has *"a single memory system, where space and time are both coded by the same engram-creating mechanism."* Which was essentially correct, since space-time data must be stored in this way. More, he even wanted to cure the diseases of the brain with his *semiconductor-based "pharmacodialysis" devices implanted in the skull* – a plan not unlike our own program that once let sea storms "implant" some bacteria in higher order cells to initiate the metamorphosis of these lives into organelles of energy: a key to evolution here.

To track the source of this curious combination of thoughts, I reconstructed Ludvig's life. His mental power spectrum was quite average, without talents for algebra or music – though he had no difficulties in going through medical school and publishing on epilepsy as student while also getting national interest with essays on art. Nor was his physical quality spectrum remarkable in any way. In his youth, as a tall soccer player with curly hair and blue eyes, he was found attractive by some females, though one reminded him: "Your mother is beautiful, but you are not".

The demands of his space-time were partly favorable to him partly against who he was.

The Space he was born to was named "Hungary": a small place in Europe, rivers and plains surrounded by mountains, found by ancient "Magyars" migrating from Asia to create a country of beauty, then were conquered and robbed often, though they survived, with a sad and confused soul compensated with surreal pride, while producing some of humankind's best, -- among the peasants, workers, soldiers and beggars who sustained and inspired them, -- the composers Liszt and Bartok; the filmmaker Huszarik; the writers Ady, Zrinyi, Attila Jozsef, Arany, Bari, Madach, who reflected this unfinished -- half-Asian, half-European -- mind; Fonyod's Csilla Molnar, embodiment of teen perfectness; the physician Semmelweis: "savior of mothers"; the lonely traveler Korosi-Csoma, who sought the land of ancient Magyars and opened, instead, Tibet to the world; the movers of mathematics, science and engineering, from the Bolyais and Kando through Bekesy, Szent-Gyorgyi, Cannon's co-author Lissak to von Neumann and the Simonyis. But they were far, very far, from Ludvig's birthplace Kaposvar: little town with little dreams.

  The Time he traversed there was also a strange one: born nine years after Nagasaki and Hitler, the air he breathed was filled with remorse, desire to renew, yearning for inspiration grown from purity. But these were difficult leads, conflicting many lives, -- a prospect for Ludvig, too, at the end of his childhood.

  His dominant social influence came from his family, a small and closed one, never rich. He loved his father, the older Nandor, descendant of Saxonian entrepreneurs settling in Transylvania, then part of Hungary, just to lose their status in the first World War, forcing the older man's mother, widowed young, to move with him and his sister Gizella to that Kaposvar. It was this town where he met as a teenager with Margit, daughter of a poor Jew, and told her: "I will marry you". Which he did, against the will of his military commander, as the next World War just started and Jews with no protection were prosecuted, most taken away to death camps. But their love and loyalty overcame the war and brought two lives to the planet: Agnes and, ten years later, this Nandor, the younger. Who loved her mother dearly too, the evenings when she listened Agnes playing Chopin on her piano – Gizella's gift -- while he watched them in silence.

When a small library opened in their street, the Pivotal Childhood Event came: he – a five-year-old! -- was asked to help to organize the books.

"These are called books, but each of them is a door to wonders multiplied by the number of people who went inside and returned" – he thought when the librarian and he finished the work. He could not have other mission than "…to experience, or at least sense, what all books hide, how their wholeness looks and sounds, not just the fruits of some, though taste good, but the oneness of all, the woods they belong to, wherever they are." But this was not achievable. Not with what he had. Deadly, as he wanted it to be "grown from purity".

The essay he wrote against "euthanasia", physician-assisted ending of human lives, was prized at his university, -- yet it was mocked because it connected thoughts from Hippocrates and the Book of Job to Schrödinger and Baudelaire. "You are talented" – told him a leading TV-man after reading his outlines for scientific shows. From the distance, Ludvig worshipped the man's sister Edit, an actress, and understood her suicide. This distance remained: the shows were blocked because of their lack of Marxist approach.

He still succeeded in science, married, immigrated to New York, published a book of poetry, had children, directed research labs, helped students to learn about neuroscience, moved beyond theories by inventing a therapeutic device, made it safe with knowledge gathered in animal studies as needed in his time, though haughty and vain, hardly likeable, he insulted 24 men and hurt 18 women – just to see his projects left without money, career boycotted, invention sidelined, marriage collapsing, futures emptied. He drove off the cliff on a starlit mountain -- "still an elegant solution if *not to be*" is the answer" -- he thought. Half-dead for three weeks, he survived, to end up in homelessness.

Was he ever happy?

Yes, he was when he dined with his father, mother and Agnes on the days of getting his degrees – sensing, finally, some traces of pride within their aura of sacrifice and love.

Yes, he was when in the first post-divorce year his little daughter Szonja dared the "snowstorm of the decade" that buried New York and went with him -- squeezing his hands on the empty streets, smiling: "What a snowy day!" -- to spend the weekend at his place. Where she also put in her subconscious domain three words that sixteen years later would move into her first legal paper, "*The Tribes Must Regulate: Jurisdictional, Environmental, and Religious Considerations of Hydraulic Fracturing on Tribal Lands*".

Yes, he was when his older daughter Laura -- from another mother, unacknowledged by him for long – accepted his invitation and met with him in the city of Krakow to see together, as she asked, Wyspianski's stained glass window "*Creation*". Where their inner closeness, meaning more than their outer distance, was revealed, just as the same soul they shared like rivers of light from the same source.

Yes, he was when -- already down and out -- checking his e-mails in a public library he finally saw a letter from Krista, his youngest daughter, *"I hope one day we can reconnect and rebuild our relationship not based on a shared love of misery and pessimism, but on creativity, excitement of new ideas, and deep observations of the world. I have forgiven you for things I was angry about from the past, I have no animosity or resentment towards you. I'm sorry if there are things that I did that hurt you, I hope you can forgive me too. Either way, I am proud to be your daughter and will always love you."*

Though I timed to send this report nineteen years from now, I rather projected these few years to transmit the stream while this man can absorb a copy.

29. A filmmaker and a programmer in Brooklyn; the "Paradiso, 1999" produced in their kitchen

New York did produce another episode I recorded with the highest resolution: the year of a pair living in the borough of Brooklyn. Claire, the woman, wanted to reconnect filmmaking to the realm of arts – a teenager dream – but with an unattractive body, fear of sex, and childhood in Wyoming, she found no man or woman of money to support her scripts. Tomio, the man, originally from Japan, left engineering school – then all jobs he could later hold -- because of his unusual form of depression, ending up as a freelance programmer, lonely, sitting at his computer eighteen hours per day. Since they lived in the same building above a grocery store and both had the strange habit of bringing up a cup of coffee from the store at midnight, after about a year Claire collected the courage to invite him to the studio her parents kept renting for her.

Tomio felt relaxed at her place; Claire's anxiety dissipated. She even said a few words about her problems as a filmmaker and that only her mother's love kept her going; Tomio mentioned his job problems related to his "mood issues" -- "atypical", he added. When he left, they agreed to repeat this Thursday midnight coffee on the following week – which they did. When Tomio came next time, he surprised Claire by asking about her scripts. She showed him her most loved one: a fantasy about the sportsman Joe DiMaggio's meeting with his actress ex-wife, Marilyn Monroe, in heaven, Dante's "Paradiso". "I know it's a strange story" – she smiled. But Tomio started to read it, sipping his coffee at the window, occasionally watching the snowfall.

Their third coffee-time was about little things: breakfast habits, grocery people, why they like to work during the night. But on the fourth, Tomio turned to Claire: "I wrote a program that cuts out moving images of actors or actresses from their original films… then it lets you alter their facial expressions, moves, the clothes they wear… and when it's done the program can insert the recreated images in other filmed backgrounds… with sounds -- I think you could use it for your movie". He even asked Claire to see how the first, "far from perfect", version worked – in the kitchen where she kept her computer. What he showed was the first two minutes of the script: DiMaggio, old and sick, is in his bed in the intensive care… it is the middle of the night… the TV screen is a blur… but he sees the date clearly… "Nineteen ninety-nine… So, this turned out to be the year to meet with Marilyn…" – says his inner voice, ending the clip. Claire, stunned, stayed in her chair; Tomio left, looked tired.

A week later Tomio brought a little device: "Claire, this has one terabyte. So you can store hundreds of films about your people.

Then I can take their moving images and make them ready to fit in the scenes you select." Though they kept meeting only for their Thursday night coffee, the images started to come together: computers and humans exchanged data, commands, inspirations, -- to breathe life into a myth.

By the end of March, Claire's screen displayed DiMaggio's memories on his last evening with Marilyn at her house: they are sitting on the floor, a bit embarrassed, talking about hardships after their divorce, planning their second wedding. Marilyn suddenly goes to her books and returns with Dante's "Paradiso", she wants to hear how it sounds in Italian, so he reads – with respect instead of surprise or annoyance -- the first lines that caught his eyes: "O luce etterna che sola in te sidi, sola t'intendi, e da te intelletta e intendente te ami e arridi!" ... Now she kisses him -- at which point the scene falls apart, gets unintelligible, mixing with Marilyn's pained look at bottles of drugs: dangerous if combined... and the same phone call is heard, again and again: "...a terrible accident... I pronounced her dead this morning..." – until the scene changes: a nurse hurries to DiMaggio to fix his hair and tubes, put his pillows in order.

In August, "Paradiso, 1999" – as it was finally titled – got the last touches in Claire's kitchen. The sequence when the dying man's vision takes him to "Paradiso" – through never-seen, beautiful landscapes, suns, interstellar clouds -- and he walks toward Marilyn, and they look at each other with the clarity and understanding so unreachable in life, turned out good, just as the scenes when they are greeted by Dante and Beatrice, yet are not surprised at all; when they meet with Jackie and Jack and receive their embrace with love, liberated from the jealousy and hatred that flowed among them back on Earth; when they see, in the lights they are crossing, Marilyn's last, unfinished letter: *"Dear Joe, If I can only succeed in making you happy, I will have succeeded in the biggest and most difficult thing there is – that is, to make one person completely happy. Your happiness means my happiness, and"* …

Before the first showing of the film, in a small club, Claire said this to Tomio: "Are you sure you know what you did? One day our program can translate language to moving images, to retake film from the grip of business, Hollywood, Bollywood, this wood, that wood, and give it to the people of truth all over the world…" But Tomio just wanted to save his good mood, the moments with strangers who were kind to him. It could not last long: within a month a big law firm sued Tomio for unauthorized use of moving images; Claire, unexpectedly called by a famous agent, found herself entangled in negotiations. Their film was never distributed.

30. The plan to build a Sphere in Antarctica; the Sphere as a palace for the Government of Earth

Will the noosphere of Claire, Tomio, their accusers, negotiators and 7.7 billion fellow humans build the site where Our World can be felt?

At least it was started, with an e-mail from an architect, Peter, left to his thoughts in a quiet office on the Australian continent. *"Dear Maya – when you asked me on the plane to Singapore about my most secret, most loved, most impossible plan, I did not want to make you, a sociologist, uncomfortable or anxious about my political views. But I now confess I do have such a plan, as bizarre as improbable, yet making sense to me, a 260-meter diameter, digitally controlled sphere of snow-melting, stainless steel framework supporting titanium and glass curtain walls with a mostly wood interior. It would be built on the safest shore of Antarctica, with supplies from stations in the southernmost places of Chile, Argentina. The sphere, a palace as pure as its environment and powered entirely by the storms there, would host the Government of Earth to harmonize the divergent interests of nations as justly as effectively, to serve all instead of the advantages of the strong, to free the planet's body and vicinity from weapons -- thus serving the centuries ahead instead of the whims of the day, thus saving Humankind's relationship with Earth. As an architect, I know how to design this sphere with its symbolism and function integrated in the beauty of the continent, and I have the colleagues to work with me free of charge, as myself, so that the costs of construction can be cut by 20% -- but you are the one who knows whether societies would welcome or ignore a plan like this."*

Maya responded a week later that she understood the symbolism of the site, "to govern humankind from the only continent untainted by sins", but in her opinion societies on Earth, still under the spell of competition for space, knowledge and resources, were not yet ready to accept this highest form of global cooperation, though she got promising feedback from friends in Chile and Argentina – likely because of the projected economic impact of those supply stations. She also wrote that *"obviously, the hardly less than 4-billion-dollar construction costs would have a prohibitive effect on the plan,"* – though assured Peter she would proceed, free of charge, with organizing the *"seemingly realistic South American component."*

An economist from Peter's wider circle also joined the project: Luis from Spain suggested to raise funds for the construction costs by using the World Wide Web, since *"by contacting only 0.5% of the planet's 7.7 billion people via the internet for donating more than 2 dollars per month over 5 years, the same amount for rich and poor, the 4.6 billion dollars covering all costs could be generated – with the donors' names to be inscribed in the steel framework so that each can be searchable and viewable from anywhere on Earth."* He warned Peter that requesting equal money from every donor, with no exception, is the *"key to prevent unwanted pressures and fights for ownership, especially from the billionaire class"* and that it must be assured that *"not a single dollar can be removed from this special – and transparent -- account by anybody for any purpose until the whole fund is deposited and construction can start."* Luis also offered to work on this without salary.

The three – Peter, Maya and Luis – soon got collaborators from the scientist community living in Antarctica: they offered to work out a complete plan for making this spherical palace *"...an environmentally acceptable self-powered structure in harmony with all living creatures of the continent."* They did not request money for their cooperation either.

Problems came when Peter approached some clinicians to explore whether any of them could afford to help to set up the necessary medical facilities in the building and eventually serve there for a year or two as volunteers. Most did not respond. Those who did, wrote Peter that since their management sees no business in this "enterprise" they "regret to inform" him about their decision of "not joining this time".

But it was easy for him to convince a few computer engineers that one of the functions of the Antarctic palace should be to control data processing in the internet, because, as he and his neuroscientist friend Paul argued, *"...from the movement and treatment of data in the World Wide Web a global mind has evolved, and just as the human mind cannot function as a healthy unit without its prefrontal assembly for morals controlling inputs and outputs, the global mind cannot function harmlessly either without a similar control system."* Two of the approached engineers, Minh from Vietnam and John from Australia, promised to elaborate on "balancing the sanctity of freedom with the rule of goodwill and adherence to truth in the Web."

A French scholar, Charles, reminded Peter that his plan is essentially about governing "the noosphere of Teilhard de Chardin", which Peter acknowledged -- then asked Charles to write an addendum to the book Maya, Luis, Paul, Minh, John, himself and a group of scientists in Antarctica were soon to publish about the project. Charles sent his addendum two weeks later, echoing Peter's and his friends' thoughts: *"Noosphere, the digital collective mind of all humans who live or passed away with footprints, is destined to be governed: to suppress its abuse, to separate truth from untruth in its data flow and move them into different subspheres, to prevent war and aggression, to let the planet's resources be available for every man and woman, to respond to attacks from Nature in the best ways, to help new communities make home in uninhabited seas, deserts and mountains – indeed, on the shores of Antarctica -- as a prelude to settlements elsewhere in the Solar System, to be prepared for the day when our intelligence is contacted by the one waiting for us."*

Maya was attacked first as the "naiveté" behind the project, "apologist for failed utopians" – jeopardizing her grants and career. Luis came next, accused with "the most sophisticated international money scam ever", bringing him into legal battles he never foresaw. Paul, Minh and John were just named as "schemers against the freedom of the internet", but it soured their relationship with the team.

Peter found himself increasingly isolated, -- then eight months after the publication of their book he died in an airplane crash. Thus, he did not see the articles about the "fundamental architectural flaws" in his design, nor the popular blog calling him a "megalomaniac bordering on comical." A thriving Russian-American company did use his – purposely unpatented -- architectural solutions for their plan to develop in Antarctica "the most unique hotel resort for the affluent with adventurous mind", quickly getting some Hollywood actors on board. They accomplished nothing besides accessing capital.

31. The plan to replace human workers with robots; global wars and mental enslavement for the replaced

If columns of snow decorated the entrance of Peter's envisioned sphere, if light greeted newcomers in Claire's Paradise, the three men whose meeting I recorded in the same decade at a ski resort on the Alps attached very different meaning to these elements: valuing snow as a wall to exclude others, prizing light as a tool for advantage, loving the two combined as key to secrecy. Still, they wasted no time.

The first man asked: "What is the latest on replacing workers with robots?"

The second man answered clearly: "Our forecast is that employment of humans in construction, transportation and mining will be fully replaced by intelligent robots within fifteen years. In agriculture, manufacturing, administration and business services this period will likely extend to twenty years. Human involvement in leisure, hospitality, information and health care services will be adjusted to equal share with robotics. We are still not sure about the optimal decrease of human resources in education. A further decrease by only thirty percent seems acceptable, and doable by promoting machine formats without human interaction. Altogether, these should result in replacing two-thirds of the human workforce with robots in two generations."

The third man now joined: "These are good figures. The time-frame is reasonable. Reducing the need for human workforce to this extent is consistent with our plans for further escalating wars in Asia and Africa. These will be executed as steps in the "clash of civilizations". Well-timed religious components will be added. Ultimately this war effort, with technologies keeping valuable infrastructure intact, should cut the world's unemployed -- useless and troublesome -- by half. But the task remains: what to do with the rest?"

Attention returned to the first man. "We anticipated this problem. At the airport, I will give you details on our self-destructing screen-card. Essentially, we argue that our future is to keep the rest of human population entertained, free to consume drugs of pleasure, practice all kinds of sex, vote for whoever politicians they like. But their classes must be kept separated, trained to be foes. Their distance from sciences, arts and morals is more crucial than ever -- past and future are not for them. And fear, administered by machined intelligence, should be their constant companion: fear from police, job loss, terrorists, bankers, humiliation in the Web -- whatever. These maintain the front we are, emerged to lead, own, influence."

Each smiled, agreed to address the control of markets for inhabitable flying spheres next time: personalized machines plus airborne infrastructure.

Then they turned and skied away, with ease and experience, one to east, one to west, one to south.

32. My challenge to the Law of Non-Interference; words for my successor on this planet

"COMPETITION AMONG FATES FOR EQUALLY ATTRACTIVE RESOURCES OF ENERGY, SPACE AND SUCCESS, YET HARMONIZING WITH THE LAW OF NON-INTERFERENCE" – human evolution was built on this thought.

None has witnessed its majesty closer than I, who recorded the waves from Lucy's necklace and Totenum's cave to Heloise's letter and Peter's sphere; saw billions of mothers nurturing their children and fathers struggling for their family, peasants bringing food to the market and workers pouring love in their goods; followed Spartacus, Washington, Gandhi fighting for freedom: separated by their worlds, connected by their essence; heard Orpheus and the child Angelina Jordan sing and Melbourne's homeless pianist, Natalie Trayling, playing on the street; watched Darwin and Wallace working on their books and Armstrong stepping with Aldrin on the planet's moon; marveled at the complex minds of Ashoka, Shakespeare and Mishima, and the way Arshile Gorky painted "The Artist and His Mother"; experienced how Moses led his people to freedom, the deaf Beethoven conducted his "Ninth", and Rosa Parks remained in her seat while a superpower commanded her to stand up.

If my reverence is missing from just one of my reports -- then all the million weigh less than a single leaf on an oak tree.

But don't we spread Life because our ancestors felt this Universe was imperfect with our lone spark? Thus, cannot the spark we ourselves created on Earth be imperfect?

I feel the answer: "Your own Tagore saw more than what you cited, saw more than the tears of gods when they discovered the loss of a star and couldn't find her! Since your priestly poet knew that "... *in the deepest silence of night the stars smile and whisper among themselves---`Vain is this seeking! unbroken perfection is over all!'*

Unbroken perfection.

Didn't the "Neanderthals" also become extinct despite their human face, hands and soul – just because they were less smart than the "sapiens"? Weren't the early Christians, poor and gentle, massacred in three continents -- just to become mass murderers themselves when got into power? Weren't 5,325 prisoners of war sacrificed on the pyramids of Aztecs in a single summer; 12,525,651 Africans forced into slavery by traders from societies stronger than theirs; 41,225,854 men's and women's life destroyed in the first World War fought for supremacy in owning the planet's resources? Didn't the politicians of Germany, when their Hitler was celebrated as the "Man of the Year" by New York's powerful, already have their plans to annihilate the Jewish people they viewed as competitors?

Didn't India's priestly class teach that human beings in lower social strata should be closed out of education, while the Marxists of China taught that "old customs, habits, culture and ideas must be destroyed" to give space to theirs? Aren't children and the young trafficked from East to West and South to North for slavery and sex, killed for their organs, or just left to die on the road if they paid already, as a spectacle for the strong in the dawn of Space Age?

This is our ancestors' plan for human evolution distorted, removed from the Soul of Multiverse. This is a force seen fully by neither Wallace nor Darwin, but channeled through Hitler: *"A stronger race will drive out the weak... to replace it by the humanity of Nature which destroys the weak to give his place to the strong."*

I do hear the thought: "Goodness can be separated from the bad only if both are experienced; without suffering the worthy cannot be revealed; fight nurtures the character, loss strengthens the mind; destruction is the twin brother of genesis. The crucifixion made Jesus, Jeanne d'Arc was reborn at the stake, Hiroshima and Nagasaki were needed to better Japan."

Were Jesus, Jeanne d'Arc, the people of Hiroshima and Nagasaki, the victims of religious sacrifices, cast systems, cultural revolutions, concentration camps, armed invasions, human trafficking, globalized slavery also asked about this in their last moment? Didn't Jesus cry out in that light of clarity: "Eloi, Eloi, lama sabachthani?"

The silent massacred couldn't even whisper these words in Jerusalem, Rome, Constantinople, Tenochtitlan, Baghdad, Paris, Wounded Knee, Nanjing, Stalingrad, Auschwitz, Katyn, Deir Yassin, My Lai, Choeung Ek, or in Srebrenica and Aleppo in the time of the World Wide Web. And those who kept their lives, with only their mission cut, derailed or taken away? One writer, Wells, devoted a sentence to them: *"All over the world, there must have been myriads of potential first-class investigators, splendid artists, creative minds, who never caught a gleam of inspiration or opportunity, for every one of that kind who has left his mark upon the world."*

    Yes, these lives – destroyed or derailed so that the evolution plan can march on Earth – were in my mind when I closed the Initial Transmission Segment with the decision of ending my existence here, "among these humans, as one of them, despite their unquenchable thirst for evil and my sky-born otherness," even if it is against the Law of Non-Interference. As I also saw humans with divine chalice in their hands, whatever the thirsts were around them. I saw their eyes close enough to know: though different, we came from the same source.

    And only my willed death – dispersing the matter of my soul and scaffold in this very orbit -- can emanate through light-years the force that challenges our Law of Non-Interference: the lines that grew from a ripple and changed the original tide, forbidding guidance for the worlds we create, leaving them on their own to thrive or perish.

Weren't we helped on our first moon by the Soul of Multiverse: unseen, distant, heavy – yet loving and patient?

Wasn't my 65 million years on this planet enough to see that human intelligence is walled in its animal past, choked by the drive to compete for resources, unable to harmonize with its mission if left alone – even if waves from the cave of Totenum and Liloen to the Voyager of Sagan and Druyan could resonate with us?

I came with my asteroid to close an imperfect path on Earth. Then let my successor open a new one, the path -- waiting to be seen for almost forty thousand years -- to which Humankind truly belongs.

If it will be opened with destruction again – even to punish the wrong, remove the occupier from the land he stole, burn down the capitals of evil, -- my successor will be nothing more than a new ruler, revengeful god, giver of judgment, last or not, for lives misled in our absence, for sins grown from our imperfectness.

Instead, Earth must be given a new continent: concentric circles of islands with a central plateau in the space of the Pacific Ocean, by using our ways to amplify geological forces, harmlessly, from our own unseen distance, and protect this new world with invisible shields letting through only the men and women of goodness, if they come, each carrying a piece of soul from the blocked, the massacred, the burned, and use the right for separation to realize Humankind's Future and devote themselves for it.

While leave those billionaires, military men, political leaders and other traffickers of people, cults and social power to complete -- with their celebrated servants and allied mob -- Humankind's Past.

Let competition for resources be replaced by cooperation in freedom to create, let this freedom harmonize with laws where "non-interference" is replaced by help from Our World when needed, interaction when asked, yielding to humans when deserved.

Let the settlers of that Pacific continent bow, when they arrive, at a new statue of liberty, a simple arch inscribed with words from neither gods misheard nor us erring creators, but from a simple man, modest as the lifeforms he studied, poor in most of his life, recognized only by a few, Alfred Russell Wallace:

"Whenever we depart from the great principles of truth and honesty, of equal freedom and justice to all men whether in our relations with other states, or in our dealings with our fellow-men, the evil that we do surely comes back to us, and the suffering and poverty and crime of which we are the direct or indirect causes, help to impoverish ourselves."

And underneath these lines, let there be twelve more words: "Men and Women are equal before the Soul that raised this arch."